CW00494467

Basil Howe
A Story of Young Love

Basil Howe

A Story of Young Love

by

Gilbert Keith Chesterton

Introduced by Denis J. Conlon

New City
London

First published in Great Britain by
New City
57 Twyford Avenue
London W3 9PZ

Illustrations:
Front cover: Courbet, G.: *Joe, the beautiful Irish girl*
Photo: © The National Museum of Art, Stockholm
Back cover: © Hulton-Deutsch Collection/CORBIS

Cover design
Tomeu Mayans

A catalogue record of this book is available from the British Library

ISBN 0 904287 73 4 Paperback
ISBN 0 904287 74 2 Hardback

Typeset in Great Britain by New City

Printed in the Czech Republic

Contents

Acknowledgements

I wish to acknowledge the assistance of Dr. Richard Christophers and Dr. Andrew J. Prescott of the British Library, and I am particularly indebted to Mr. Aidan Mackey for first alerting me to the existence of those of Chesterton's notebooks which had long lain forgotten under articles of clothing in an old box trunk.

D. J. Conlon

BASIL HOWE,
THE BACKGROUND

Introduction

After the death in 1989 of Dorothy Collins, Gilbert Chesterton's secretary from 1926 to 1936, the Chesterton papers were sold to the British Library for £200,000 provided out of funds from the bequest of GKC's old debating opponent, Bernard Shaw. The papers, kept in an attic study at Miss Collins's Top Meadow Cottage in Beaconsfield since the death of Frances Chesterton in 1939, were being prepared for shipment when an old chest, always thought to contain academic gowns, mortarboards and related items fell open. The state of the clothing was not good, in fact it was extremely musty after the passing of half a century, but a tentative rummage revealed that beneath lay an unforeseen find: dozen upon dozen of notebooks, old school exercise books and loose papers. Upon the death of his mother in 1933, Chesterton had thrown out a collection of his works made by his father; although much was lost to the municipal tip, Dorothy Collins had arrived to scoop up what papers remained and taken them to Beaconsfield. It was obvious that the two hundred notebooks were what had survived.

Later examination and a cross-check with Miss Collins's card index revealed that some attempt had been made to catalogue them in the 1930s, but the titles then affixed did not always reflect what was within and sometimes were quite misleading. No doubt in time this would have been remedied, but Chesterton's death in 1936, followed by his wife's illness and death in 1939, and then the outbreak of war, saw first the removal of the papers from Top Meadow to the neighbouring Top Meadow Cottage, and then the cottage (in fact, a very substantial house) used as an annexe to St. Joseph's Nursing Home for women evacuated from the city to have their babies in what were hoped would be safer surroundings; Miss Collins drove an ambulance. It was hardly surprising that, after the cessation of hostilities, a chest that had been crammed with unwanted items of clothing and pushed into the loft lay long forgotten. The confused situation was compounded by either Frances Chesterton or Dorothy Collins having attempted to form an index by removing title pages and putting them all together in one folder; this no doubt worked as long as there was a survivor who could relate a title page to a particular work, but by 1989 there was nobody to do so and in fact many title pages had been lost, or, where title pages survived, the works had disappeared. This situation must have already existed in the 1930s, since Miss Collins, apparently without reading them, classified the two parts of this present book as separate stories under the titles "Valentine Amiens" and "The History of Three Babies"; the prologue and first chapter were eventually found as loose papers, but the title page remains elusive, and so we have chosen to call Chesterton's first novel *Basil Howe*.

The two exercise books containing the narrative are written in Chesterton's early mature hand writing which was to be replaced by an italic hand which he adopted soon after he began his studies at University College, London and the Slade School of Art, where from 1893 until 1895 he trained as a book illustrator; this suggests that *Basil Howe* was written in late

1893 or early 1894. Like many other first novels Chesterton's story of the developing love between a gauche and lanky young man and a fiery, free-spirited red-headed girl seems to have a strong autobiographical undertow. Both date and autobiographical content are confirmed by another story entitled *Our Future Prospects*, a fictitious account of what happened to the members of the Junior Debating Society of St. Paul's School after they had left their alma mater. Although the JDC at St. Paul's seems not to have survived the departure of Chesterton and his friends, their particular group continued to meet quite regularly, hold an annual JDC dinner, and appear as a group at St. Paul's reunions until the early 1950s when advancing age finally took its toll.

Our Future Prospects is firmly dated 16th June 1894 and its form suggests that each of the members was intended to contribute a chapter which guyed the other members and placed the one destined to write the following chapter in a predicament which was to be solved by his ensuing literary effort. Chesterton seems to have acted as clearing house by making good copies, adding illustrations and then passing on the narrative. This process came unstuck at some point and the story after Chapter VII was apparently never returned; a long note written many years later in what appears to be E. C. Bentley's hand gives rise to the suspicion that he was the guilty party.

The part of *Our Future Prospects* relevant to *Basil Howe* is the meeting, love affair and marriage of Gilbert Chesterton and a red-headed cousin of Bentley's called Gertrude Grey. The thrust of the narrative is, of course, nonsense but it is obvious that the members of the Junior Debating Club are familiar with

Gertrude Grey and do not find it amiss that she should marry a tall shy young man (as he then was) called Chesterton. In other words, they had all read *Basil Howe* and assumed that the eponymous hero was none other than the chairman of the JDC. In later years, after Chesterton's death, Maisie Ward, when writing her biography, did consult members of the JDC but seems not to have enquired too deeply into their knowledge of GKC's early life and loves, relying largely on what she was told by Frances Chesterton (not on the scene until at least 1896 and known to be almost pathologically afraid of any aspect of her life appearing in print)[1] and Dorothy Collins, GKC's Secretary from 1926-36. It seems unlikely in any case that Chesterton would ever have regaled his wife with tales of his teenage loves, and Miss Collins would have had no knowledge of events of over thirty to forty years before, and the JDC, who knew the identity of Gertrude Grey, had either forgotten all about her or saw little point in reviving memories of what they probably considered an innocent and inconsequential liaison. Miss Collins, when questioned by later biographers, tended to suggest that GKC's early writings depicted E.C. Bentley in the figure of the slim young man (in fact there is one short account in which both Bentley and Chesterton figure), but it must be remembered that she had only known Chesterton as the immense, twenty-odd stone figure of his later years, whereas Bentley had remained lean throughout his life.

Much of Chesterton's early fiction was loosely based on the characters of his friends, many of whom appear suitably disguised in tales such as *The Human Club* (which title was adopted by his friends for their meetings when they went up to Oxford) and *Wine of Cana*.

Alongside them also appears a group of girls, usually a trio of sisters, sometimes given fictional names but occasionally identified as the Vivian sisters who lived down the street in Warwick Gardens in Kensington:

> "I have never been able, in fact I have never tried to tell which of the three I really liked best, and if the severer usefulness and domesticity of the eldest girl, with her quiet art-colours, and broad, brave forehead as pale as the white roses that clouded the garden, if these maturer qualities in Nina demanded my respect more than the levity of the others, I fear they did not prevent me feeling an almost equal tide of affection towards the sleepy acumen and ingrained sense of humour of Ida, the second girl and book-reader for the family; or *Violet, a veritably delightful child with a temper as formless and erratic as her tempest of red hair."* (early 1890s)[2]

As Ada Chesterton, Gilbert's sister-in-law and colleague, noted: "the fugitive heroines who occasionally flit through his stories are inevitably red-headed ... red hair signified to Gilbert beauty and romance."[3] Be that as it may, within a couple of years of describing Violet Vivian's temper and red hair, Chesterton was describing the self-same temper and hair in the person of Gertrude Grey in *Basil Howe*, and his friends were gently ribbing him in *Our Future Prospects*. Perhaps it is also worth noting that the first encounter in *Basil Howe* appears to occur in Lyme Regis, a resort for which Chesterton always retained fond memories and which he continued to visit for the rest of his life. And yet, within two years of the composition of *Basil Howe*, Gilbert Chesterton was to leave University College, go to work as a publisher's illustrator and reader, and, apparently romantically unattached, be introduced in 1896 to his future wife, Frances Blogg, at a discussion group in Bedford Park. By coincidence, Frances Blogg was also one of three sisters but her hair was brown in colour; Chesterton would seem to have recycled a few poems by changing the name of his lady-love, but it is also within the bounds of possibility that he did the same with *The Appalling Five*, an early version of *The Man Who Was Thursday*, which is only extant in an unfinished copy made in Frances's hand: in it the heroine's hair is brown, although when *Thursday* was published in 1907 its heroine again had flaming red hair. What had happened to Violet Vivian/Gertrude Gray? No-one now seems to know what happened to the Vivian sisters and their family; at the time when it would have been possible to find out there was no need to do so, as everyone probably knew. We are left with a` possible clue in a love poem from another of those notebooks dating from the 1890s, a poem so full of nostalgia and of separation in love that it suggests that the Vivians had moved some considerable distance away, far enough to put an insurmountable barrier between a young man yet to make his way in the late Victorian world and the young woman whom he was in no financial position to ask for her hand in marriage:

Again

Like the wind on the sands she was in the flare
of her sand-wild hair,
Like to a gull in the foam she was, like to a
rushing of air;

*Billowed and brake her flaming locks 'gainst the
dreaming blue of the sea,
Like to a dash of a sudden rain, like to a flood went she.*

*And I, I followed fleetly, how could I follow but fleet,
For the sea went by in her great wild eyes, and
the sea-wind in her feet,
And the long wave rose as an elfin wall and bent
as a flickering crown,
And a russet cloudland barred the night when
the broad red sun went down.*

*Many a maiden lingers, with poppy-fans at her feet,
When the swallows dapple the yellow dome, and
the slopes are ribbed with wheat,
But at her feet, jaggèd and fiery only the starfish lay,
And above her head with a clamour the hoarse
gull rushed astray.*

*She looked on the cliff and the shingles, she stood
by the surfs and me,
She moved 'twixt the rock and the raucous wave,
a very child of the sea.
The morning wasted the shorelands, one morning
emptied the grot;
Morning she came unto me; one morning came she not.*

*Life went on with its duties, gatherings, questions, strife,
On through the long year's roaring; and she sank
out of my life.
And I sealed up my heart with portals, walls without
crevice or mark,
But within my heart lay an ocean whose pulses
throbbed in the dark.*

And some hour of the year, in the darkness whose sun
was barred in a grave,
Would break with a sudden thunder a long white
desolate wave.
And the good friends gathered round me, the true,
the tender, the strong,
The brave old band of comrades I have loved
so well and long,

And they trod my heart as a meadow, a windy
wandering heath,
And the young-eyed daisies showed not the old
earth-grave beneath.
One morning a word fell vaguely: she was coming,
perchance was nigh.
How lightly the chance was taken on the lips of
others than I!

A knocking: a door half-opened, a shape – and
from that hour down
A dazzling fire and a fragrance: a sudden secret crown.
In the grey of a parlour twilight mine eyes could but
heavily see –
If God's strong world be not as a dream – it was
not a dream, but she

With her high head low for a greeting, her proud
cheeks fair with a flame,
Speaking clear in the gloaming, simply saying my name.
After the long years, fruitful, strong, after the love
gains won,
After the slow births, mighty and new, that now
seemed little and done,

After the broad lands, noisy and thronged, that
lay 'twixt me and the sea,
God, who forgets not what he has willed, looked
on us, I and she.
She sat yet again beside me; a fire sang in my head;
We said things childish, frantic. Who knows what
things we said?

In jest and story and rhyming, memory, fancy, game?
I looked on her great eyes ever to find them ever
the same.
She went to a drear piano, laughing dreamily slow,
And she played the old song, senseless, sweet,
that she sang to me long ago.

And I scarce spake, vaguely deeming rankèd
angels looking on,
That I might do nought unworthy of the great
thing God had done.
We had our smile and we parted. I held her hand
and she went,
But my heart had wakened within me with
meaning and high intent:

It was not ended in childhood; it was not buried
in sand.
God spake and set us there once again, for a
moment, hand in hand.
It may be God shall will me lost love and a
lonely chair:
God works no woe of the dusty world that a brave
man may not bear.

But thorns be crowns or roses, loss be in lot or gain,
The old sea-dream was something. I have lived
to see her again. (B.L., 73324 A).

It would be idle to speculate as to how far this poem is based on reality and how far *Basil Howe* is an exercise in wish fulfilment, but an unhappy outcome to a love affair might help to explain the gloomy solipsism into which Chesterton fell for a time between 1893 and 1896. That bout of self-centred pessimism is very much at odds with the later popular image of a jolly optimistic beer-swilling GKC, who in fact rarely drank anything other than Burgundy and whom Borges thought "restrained himself from being Franz Kafka"; in like fashion, if *Basil Howe* were published anonymously, Chesterton is not the first person who would spring to mind as its author. Other fragments written about the same time confirm the style and some of the personages can be identified, Valentine Amiens being based on Robert Vernède the poet who died in the First World War and whose obituary was written by Chesterton. What seems to have inspired Chesterton to write a romantic novel at the age of twenty was first love, and into it he poured all his emotions. He would never quite do this dance of the seven veils again, for in the future at least one veil was to be kept in place to hide his private life, and yet always peeping through came the lost love's red hair which in story after story, carrying its Celtic connotation of fairy magic, bedecked those men and women who were deemed to be the inspiration of life. Perhaps, instead of wondering at Chesterton as *Basil Howe*, we should remember the anecdote that tells of every fat man having a thin man inside him fighting to get out.

1. "I have a horror greater than any other ... I loathe print. Perhaps I have too much of it, but it is a dangerous business always." Aidan Mackey: "Diary of Frances Chesterton, 1904-1905", *The Chesterton Review XXV, No.3*, August 1999.

2. B.L., 73325 A. (f.35v).

3. Mrs Cecil Chesterton (aka Keith Prothero): *The Chestertons*, London (Chapman & Hall) 1941, p 38.

THE JUNIOR DEBATING CLUB, 1891

E.W. Fordham Digby d'Avigdor

Lawrence Solomon Waldo d'Avigdor

L.R.F. Oldershaw G. K. C. B.N. Langdon-Davies

The Junior Debating Club of St. Paul's School

In 1890 a remarkable group of boys founded a Junior Debating Club at St. Paul's School in Hammersmith. At first it met weekly for tea and buns in the home of one or another of the members, but soon it was publishing a magazine, *The Debater*, devoted to their discussions and proceedings. Almost all the boys were to make their mark in later life, but not the least surprising aspect of the JDC was that the group picked as chairman a clumsy and exceedingly tall boy, Gilbert Chesterton, considered by his masters to be devoid of most talents. Nonetheless, he was soon to win the school French prize and submit a prize poem devoted to St. Francis Xavier. The influence of the JDC on its members was such that they were bound together for life, meeting at least annually, usually for dinner, until the 1950s, one meeting in 1948 at the Great Western Hotel being the occasion of the presentation of a bust of Chesterton to the alma mater. The JDC introduced its members to the skills of debating and writing which they were to develop further in later life. One of the most interesting fruits of their collaborations is *Our Future Prospects*, an account of a meeting held on 16th June 1894, a year after Chesterton had left St. Paul's School for University College, London: an innocent inquiry as to the intended careers of the members produced fanciful contributions and projections, and it would seem that the intention was for each member to supply a chapter. All seems to have gone well until it was passed to E.C. Bentley, by then at Oxford, no doubt for him to insert his contribution before returning the manuscript to

Chesterton who had editorial control; this he failed to do and the manuscript was only returned many years later with his footnote eulogising GKC. The narrative, as a result, lacks those parts of the tale to be supplied by other Debaters destined never to be able to put each other on various hooks, so the main party is stuck in the Himalayas and Maurice Solomon marooned on a desert island for ever. The quality of the narrative is variable, depending on the particular writers, but what there is of the story is instructive in outlining a relationship between Chesterton and Gertrude Grey; the glimpse of Chesterton's future afforded by his fellow Debaters showing that it was taken for granted that they would marry. The same impression is conveyed very strongly in *Basil Howe* (1893-4) and it seems likely either that the Debaters were familiar with the novel or that they knew of a real life relationship between Chesterton and his red-headed girl.

Members of the Junior Debating Club

Gilbert Chesterton (Geke), Chairman of the Junior Debating Club.

Lucien Oldershaw, Secretary of the JDC, later President of the Oxford Union and OUDS, journalist, politician, academic and Chesterton's brother-in-law.

Edmund Clerihew Bentley, Librarian of the Junior Debating Club, later journalist *(Daily Telegraph)*, author (*Trent's Last Case*, etc) and creator of the clerihew.

Lawrence Solomon, later Professor of Latin, University College London.

Edward W. Fordham, later a barrister.

Bernard Noel Langdon-Davies, later a lecturer and Literary Consultant.
Digby d'Avigdor.
Waldo d'Avigdor, later director, Alliance Insurance Co.
Robert E. Vernède, poet, died in battle 1917.
Francis George Lawder Bertram, later Director of Civil Aviation, Air Ministry.
Maurice Solomon (Grey), later Director, General Electric Company.
Hubert Arthur Sams, later Director General of the Indian Post Office. The only member of the JDC to be knighted (as forecast in *Our Future Prospects*).
Frederick R. Salter, later Chesterton's solicitor (Salter & Lees).
Leonard Magnus.

Peile - an (unloved ?) teacher at St. Paul's School.

Our Future Prospects
as written by the Junior Debating Club

Prologue

> 'Come now, let us meet
> Tomorrow morn once more in one full field
> Of gracious pastime, that once more the King
> Before ye leave him for this quest, may count
> The yet unbroken strength of all his knights,
> Rejoicing in the order that he made.'
>
> ***The Holy Grail***

A meeting of the Junior Debating Club was held on Friday June 16th, 1894. Host Mr. Vernède.

Mr. Fordham read a paper on *Our Future Prospects*. It was his opinion that of all the questions which had darkened and commonly perplexed our several childhoods, none had exceeded that commonly propounded in the words "Well – What are you going to be?" (This remark, being conveyed in the well-known tones of the distinguished public school High-Master, elicit[ed] storms of merriment.) He thought that a child of tender years and immature intellect could in no case be expected to be endowed with the fire of prophetic vision in the way suggested by the question. With us (the Debaters) however, who were already falling into the sear and yellow leaf (at this point Mr. Langdon Davies evinced a disposition to dandle Mr. Maurice Solomon, a flash of the almost extinct Adam that had to be sternly checked by the chairman), with us it was so far different that we might well have gained sufficient experience of the sin and sorrow of the world as to make it possible for us (Mr. Bentley in sepulchral tones:) to foreswear it for ever.

Mr. Fordham expresses a desire that Bentley shouldn't cheek and says that he doesn't want any insolence, and shortly proceeds – to appreciate its probable effect upon ourselves.

Chapter I. A Country-house

Young Sir Guyon proudly said
Love shall never be my fate.
'None can say so but the dead!'
Shrieked the witch-wife at his gate.
Stopford Brooke

In the front hall of that peculiar paradise and happy hunting-fields of the modern novelist which we notice in the title of this chapter, a grave-looking young man with pince-nez, who was not, in his own eyes at least, a fitting ornament to an amatory romance, was engaged in endeavouring to remember the names of his cousins, to whom he was being introduced. With the younger of the two, a girl of 17 by name Dorothy, he had indeed had some previous friendship, so that he saluted her with a shade less portentous solemnity than he thought fit to extend to his general recognition of the ties of kinship. As he was, a few moments afterwards, being conducted through the garden which was as the heralds would say, *semé* of curates and young ladies, he was startled and shaken from his customary severity of demeanour by the sight of a tall and particularly untidy looking young man, who could hardly be said to belong to either of the two above categories. Making his way to him with a peculiar silent swiftness of which he was capable, he held out his hand, observing "Chesterton, if I may quote the fine expression of Locke, how do you do?" The tall and untidy turned sharply and his face betrayed more pleasure than is usual in the vicinity of country curates, though his words were somewhat abrupt, "Bentley, how on earth did you come here?"

"Oh, by the old way: you needn't say anything about it, you know; but the pantry window being open and the plate-basket perfectly accessible, I naturally –"

One of those mysterious assisting aunts, a species I believe peculiar to hospitable gatherings, swept up at this moment and declared that she must positively introduce her two guests to the new curate. That reverend gentleman, who was a stalwart, brown-eyed, comparatively sensible-looking reverend gentleman, was engaged in decorous and serious converse with a ring of young ladies of a parochial turn of mind, to which society, despite both his sanctity and his sense, he was not altogether impervious. No sooner, however, had this apostle beheld the two young guests approaching than a sudden and singular change came over his countenance and he startled his company by vociferating in a loud and cordial tone "Hullo Geke." The ladies stared at each other at this peculiar transformation of demeanour and it became rapidly plain to the whole assembly that the Rev. Edward Fordham needed no introduction.

"What's become of Langdon-Davies?" was the first question propounded by the individual addressed as Geke.

"Haven't a rotted – that is, a ghost of a notion," replied the curate in measured tones, "I believe he's gone to Belgium or Tunis – to what you call him, sell himself about the place, you know, and join the army."

"Am I to understand," enquired Bentley, "from your words that our poor friend has sold himself to the arch enemy or (remembers he is talking to a curate but scorns to flinch) the devil?"

The curate laughed uneasily. "No: not yet, that I know of: but the fact is the last I heard from him was that he thought of taking a commission in some continental army or something. Here, Geke, let me introduce you, Mr. Chesterton, to Miss Dorothy Grey, Miss Gertrude Grey."

Mr. Chesterton shakes hands with two young ladies, one dark and the other indescribably chestnut-haired, who proceed to make some very witty remarks about the weather. No mortal man ever contrived to talk to two ladies at once for more than five minutes, so that in the end Bentley finds himself in the company of his cousin Dorothy whose friendship he values, as being the only lady present who can see the humorous side of curates. It will be apparent to all healthy-minded novel-readers for what purpose these circumstances and characters are ultimately destined, and it is, therefore, necessary to explain at once the peculiar and, we flatter ourselves, novel principle upon which we shall conduct these matters. The compilers of this prophetic history having no personal experience to go upon in the matter of love-making, and finding the minute description of the question particularly repugnant at present, propose to represent all *bona fide* love-passages by the insertion of stars. This will leave the mental filling up of details to those so inclined, and permit youth and innocence to get on the more rapidly to the more congenial passages of danger, hatred and destruction.

There follows a note in E.C. Bentley's hand. It seems implicit that Bentley should have finished the chapter, failed to do so, and then added the note some ten years later:

The gentleman above introduced as Mr. Chesterton was one of those people who have a habit of being clever, and was by way of being a genius. From his earliest years he had talents for drawing and writing poetry, which manifested themselves at the opening stages of his career at St. Paul's School on his lesson book and writing-paper. He had then become chairman of the Junior Debating Club. It was at this point that his literary work came to be regarded as promising, a series of his contributions to a small private magazine, the *Debater*, attracting the notice of several persons, who strongly advised him [to] send his poetry to magazines which would make it public. He had then left St. Paul's School and gone to various art-schools, and at the time of writing this story he was regarded as an artist of exceptionally brilliant prospects, and his papers upon various subjects in magazines, as well as two small volumes of poetry, had awakened enthusiastic feelings in the bosoms of many reviewers. In fact, Mr. Chesterton came dangerously near to being a "coming man", and only escaped that stigma by his offensive and overweening modesty, which forbade him to publish more than one-tenth part of what he wrote, while it caused him to be affected in the most painful manner when anybody ventured to speak to him of his work. His praises, at the outset, had been mainly chanted by two of his friends, one of whom we already know as Mr. Bentley, who was a Barrister, and who occasionally disgraced his nature and his name by writing articles in papers and reviewing books. The other was a Mr. Oldershaw, who had begun a journalistic career of great promise, and who, together with Mr. Bentley, started what the latter called "the G.K.C. Riots"; in other words, they succeeded in producing an immense enthusiasm about the aforesaid volumes of poems, which had left Mr. Chesterton with a reputation; this Mr. Bentley occasionally stimulated by inserting in the reviews, such as, "We hear on good authority that Mr. Chesterton, the New Poet, has in preparation an important work, which is to deal with", etc., etc. The "New Poet"'s poems were eagerly sought after, and Mr. Oldershaw published long critical articles entitled "Gilbert Chesterton, Poet and Artist", "Gilbert Chesterton and his Work", and similar headings.

Chapter II. The Moths and the Candle

> We have seen thee, O Love, thou art fair, thou art goodly, O Love.
> Thy wings make light in the air, as the wings of a dove:
> But twain go forth with thee, a man and a maid,
> Her eyes are the eyes of a bride whom delight makes afraid,
> As the breath in the buds that stir in her bridal breath,
> But fate is the name of her, and his name is Death.
>
> ***Swinburne***

"We needn't go and dress yet," said Bentley in response to the restless appeal of his companion, a slight dark young man with melancholy eyes; "it isn't 7 yet."

Mr. Vernède, the rising poet and littérateur, glancing gloomily at the clock, is obliged to admit that there is plenty of time and begins to fight with the mantlepiece ornaments, and then to walk about the room. "So Chesterton has gone on with his wife to Russia?"

"I believe," replied the other poking the fire, "that he has for once told the truth in saying so. He said he was going and I suppose he wouldn't leave his wife behind. Those whom Fordham hath joined, let no man sunder."

"Well," said the poet, sadly "I don't grudge it him of course – but –"

"But you wish you had it. So do I."

Vernède laughed, cast down as he was, "I shouldn't think you were looking forward to a honeymoon."

The barrister's brows winced and knitted and he gave a curious little laugh, far from hilarious, and stood staring at the embers.

"As for me," went on Vernède, "You know the fool's state I am in: but fool or no fool I will have it over. This evening she will be there. It is best to have it over though I don't stand the ghost of a chance." Bentley looked curiously at him, "Oh, you think not," he said.

"No," said the poet, quite honestly, for despite his languid and contemptuous mien, he was one of the few people who was really without conceit.

"Very well, then," said Bentley, with a strange short laugh, "we will go and dress."

The ball at Mr. Vincent Beauchamp's, whose daughter Vera was the subject of the above remarks, saw the advent of the two companions in the course of a few hours: in which they gyrated for some time before they got a sight of Miss Vera herself. Vernède cared very little for dancing, thinking, like the chairman, that there were other ways of testifying respect for a lady besides regarding her as a spinning top. Bentley treated dancing as he did most things, with a few exceptions, he scoffed at it and did it well. After a few dances and the proper repetition of observations about the heat of the room, they came in an interval of the Fakir ritual, into full view of Miss Vera Beauchamp, dark, keen-looking and high-coloured, leaning on the arm of a bald-headed, weak-eyed old military man with a blue ribbon, not of total abstenance. Vera was one of those types of English beauty among the choicest of the upper circles whose patrician lot it is to pose and leer and look like bad actresses and be thus presented, through the medium of the photographer, to the common herd. It may be in consequence of this duty to society, that her ordinary demeanour, though well-bred, was rather severe, for she had a heart, and some had even suspected her of some fleeting remnant of a conscience. She gave her hand to Mr. Bentley, whom she knew well as one of the rising barristers of the day, with almost masculine coolness and good-nature, but when Vernède held out his, she shrank for the quickest flash, as from a sin, and then saluted him slowly. As she turned away, on the arm of the sleepily polite General Peile, Vernède saw a face he knew, turned like his in still and watchful passion upon the woman. It was Lieutenant Bertram, a tall dark-browed, young officer under the General's command, and it may be doubted whether at that moment his were feelings of unmixed loyalty and adoration to his commanding officer: ungenerous they certainly were not, for he never was so in his life. Bentley turned to greet him, and was received with a stately smile and bow, and when he looked for Vernède, he saw that he had gone in pursuit of his lady, resolved on bringing matters to a climax. Suffice it to say, that, half an hour afterwards, they stood before the fire in the library where, after some sentence or two which our before-mentioned principles would not permit us to deal with, without having resort to the asterix, Vernède looking humbly down at the fire, stammering and speaking slowly in his speech, but looking all the more magnificent in the real bravery and honesty of his temper, offered her his life. The girl did not betray a tinge of surprise, seeming to have expected what was coming and to have hardened her heart. She stood staring at the fire, with her nostrils dilated and her eyes hot and fierce, as if she scorned herself and the world. Then her answer came in a hard, though courteous, voice.

"When you know the truth, Mr. Vernède, you may think what you like of me, but you will not blame the answer I am about to give you. Each person forms wishes, but there are too many people in the world, for some not to be snapped in the tangle. I am just engaged to General Peile."

Vernède rather wildly bowed and turned to go.

"I must say good-bye." She went, turning suddenly and her face thrown into shadow had grown sharply passionate. "I hope that you will write more and teach the world some good. There is very little good in it." Vernède bowed again and went out without a word. When he had gone a little way he came blindly against Bentley. That philosopher looked at him quickly and then led him out into the conservatory and, getting him some coffee, got him to sit down.

He did not worry the patient with questions though he knew well that the darkness of disappointment was round him: and at last Vernède broke out. "What is there of any earthly use to me?" said he bitterly.

"Why, if you will permit me, there is myself," said Bentley, "I know what is the matter. I held it truth, and you too at one time, that men rise on stepping stones of their dead selves to higher things: and I know that we shall be the better for everything yet, if we only go, as you do, undishonoured: come what may, you know you have some friends who know what you are worth: and believe me, that is the best..."

So, for a quiet hour or two, did the barrister brighten and set in order the chaotic despair poured out by the fallen lover, not the first hour of the kind that scoffer had passed in such missions. Little did either of them suppose as they talked that the woman who had dealt the blow sat before the fire fuming and choking with fierce sobs as she laughed madly at all the world. She had sold herself, at her mother's orders, and now the world was a market... if not worse. As she moved away, a tall, high-textured young man in evening dress offered her his arm. She knew him as Digby d'Avigdor, an officer in the Carbiniers, and went with him through the empty hall.

"Shall we go into the drawing room?" she said, quite calmly.

"If you will," he replied, politely, "but it hardly matters. It is so late now."

"Ah yes," she said, laughing abruptly, "it is too late now: nothing matters much now."

Chapter III. Lieutenant Bertram

> But what will God say? "Oh my sweet:
> Think and be sorry you did this thing.
> Though earth were unworthy to feel your feet,
> There's a heaven above may deserve your love."
> Should you forfeit heaven for a snapt gold ring
> And a promise broken over it just or meet?
>
> ***Browning (The Worst of It)***

Some three months after the incidents of the last chapter Lieutenant Bertram, returning from an evening at the house of Mr. H.A. Sams, M.P., one of the rising stars of British commerce, was led by a gloomy fascination to call at the house of General Peile ostensibly to return a book which he had borrowed from that newly-married victim. Report, flying through the city, did not speak highly of the peace and happiness of the household; it whispered of noisy authority and brow-beating from the perplexed husband, of savage taunts, unwomanly, almost non-human from the wife, who began to relax her melancholy pride and become, in society, more gay and reckless every day: her character becoming chaotic and complex like that of a maniac. Of this, as well as of the ringing outburst of hate which had shaken the household that very morning, Bertram knew nothing, but knocked calmly at the door where he had spent many brilliant evenings. The thing that struck him first as the door was opened by a stern servant, was the darkness of everything. Having seen that hall and those rooms twenty times, filled with lights and ball-dresses, he started at the dim candle, the barred shutters and the dark rooms, wondering what it could mean. The servant was about to give a hasty "not at home" when he saw the General come quickly out of one room towards another, and his face was livid and gaping like a corpse. He stopped when he saw Bertram, for even at that awful moment in his life his manners would not allow him to pass, and he held out a hand that twitched and shook convulsively. The other grasped it and broke out into some incoherent words of query. "Come in," said Peile hoarsely, "come in." He led him into the drawing room, strangely desolate and neglected.

"Lieutenant Bertram," he said in a weak voice, "I cannot find my wife: she is gone."

Bertram took his leg off the fender and the stir and noise echoed through the silent room.

"She has gone away," went on the General, his voice seeming to lose itself, "in a cab, across London – and –"

"We must go after her," broke in Bertram, who was a man of action much more than his commander, "Whatever her reason she must not go unprotected across the city." And he took his hat.

"That is not all," said the other, trembling and with a frightful oath, "She is not unprotected."

There was a silence and Bertram raised a face, stricken white of a sudden. "Who is he?" he cried, with a loud voice.

The pale General ground his teeth, "I do not know."

"Where did they start?"

"From the Granham livery, an hour ago."

Bertram dashed to the door and turned, "Rest certain… I will bring her back to you – and –" and his voice broke into an oath, the first that ever was on his lips. "I will meet this devil and kill him."

Ten minutes afterwards he stood before the wondering groom demanding who had left at that hour.

"There was a tall man with a lady," answered the man slowly.

"Yes, yes. Do you know them?"

"No, sire. But Davies does."

"Where is he? Ask him."

"Hi, Davies!"

"Well?" came in an aggravated voice out of the darkness.

"Who was it left with the lady at 12?"

There was a silence during which Bertram stood chafing, and then came the answer, "Lieutenant d'Avigdor of the Carbiniers."

Bertram took one step back, and then called for horses to follow.

Chapter IV.

> For front to front in an hour we stood,
> And a million horrible bellowing echoes broke
> From the red-ribbed hollow behind the wood
> And thundered up to heaven the Christian code
> That must have life for a blow.
>
> ***Maud***

Out of a room in the best hotel at Coblentz a fashionably dressed Englishman, introduced everywhere as Lieutenant Digby, was leading a dark and harrassed young lady towards the garden just after sunset, when a waiter appeared at his elbow and told him that a gentleman wished to see him. Leaving Vera Peile, for such she was, upon a seat, he turned to the door again where he saw the white face of a dark-haired, square-jawed young man in a travelling dress, and stepped back with the word "Bertram" on his lips.

"Yes," replied the other, shortly, "you can guess what I am come after."

"Indeed I cannot. But I am glad you are come," said d'Avigdor cordially, for he was really pleased to meet his old companion.

Bertram looked at him darkly. "I am come," he said, "to take back Mrs. Peile."

D'Avigdor jumped off the table and came round to him with clenched hands. "What is all this ?" he cried.

"Lieutenant d'Avigdor," said the other, "you are a worthless scroundrel!"

D'Avigdor threw his head up and looked at the speaker hard. "Well, Bertram," he said, quite sincerely, "I won't call you a liar, because I know that personally you are not, but a better man than I am: but I can with the utmost honesty accommodate by calling you a fool. My dear fellow, I am a soldier and a man of the world, and you know what words like yours mean. If you see any good in men murdering each other for a word for which the law wouldn't fine them, see it. I have been in three duels and I haven't seen the good yet."

"I have been in no duels," said Bertram, breathing hard, "I thought them wrong: but before you I think different. Profligate, traitor, wrecker of honest lives, if the law cannot give me a sword I will take one. If you will not fight for a word, fight–" and he laid his grasp upon the other's coat. D'Avigdor struck him off, with a loud oath, and stepped back.

"Tomorrow then," he said, "you idiot."

"Very well," said Bertram and sat down, flushed and fierce.

“How did you know I was here?” said the other, good-humoredly, as he stood before the fire, for he was now perfectly composed.

“Wherever you were, in whatever land or city, I would have found you,” said Bertram.

D’Avigdor looked sharply round.

“Wherever you are, in whatever land or city”: those were the words, now unconsciously repeated, which the chairman had used asking them not to lose sight of each other, to keep up the friendship in after-life: all the old time seemed before him again, debates, committees, struggles, brave loyalty in continual subscription, common brotherhood in frequent honours: to be kept up, if possible…*Vanitas vanitatis*, here was his first meeting with a comrade. He turned pale and bitter to the door, when Bertram started behind him. Into the room had strolled another young man in evening dress; he was older and taller now, but there was no mistaking the eyeglass, the thick roof of hair, the “don’t care a damn expression” as Langdon-Davies had called it: it was Bentley.

“Hullo,” he said looking from one to the other, “Bertram, d’Avigdor. Why these grim looks? Have you been talking politics or theology, or are they barred?”

“A more serious subject than those, Bentley,” said d’Avigdor mournfully enough.

“Listen to me, Bentley,” cried Bertram, who had sprung to his feet. “Thank God I have found an honest man in this cursèd nest of gadflies. You will be my second.”

“Your second” (with wild contempt). “Whom against?”

D’Avigdor bowed, “I have received Lieutenant Bertram’s challenge, and I ask no better arbiter than yourself.”

Bentley looked from one to another again. "Is this the New Humour?" he asked, "Or have I the honour to be the object of those observances to which the Church has dedicated the first of April?"

D'Avigdor laughed, but the cloud was still on his brow. "The shorter the business is the better," he said. "I like it as little as you do. Bertram has insulted me and I passed it; he has struck me, and by God I will fight. There is the long and short of the matter."

"But I thought," said Bentley, hesitatingly and with the air of an historian, "that the law of trial by battle was removed from the statute book."

"I will fight," broke in Bertram. "I say I will fight. This infamous dastard has taken his friend's wife: and I will kill him or be killed," he cried violently, for the spirit of wrath, angel or devil, was on him.

D'Avigdor was perfectly proud and quiet, and turned to Bentley, adding, "We must fight."

Bentley laughed briefly, "Nonsense," he said, "sit down like friends, or go your ways like honest men, and rational supporters of the laws against murder and riot. How would you like to go home to Chesterton and Solomon and say, "Oh, I met one Debater. I murdered him. Shall we elect another member? No bloodthirsty superstition in the world should ever make me forget the friendship and old time. Nor will it you."

D'Avigdor was staring, wild-eyed, into the fire, and his colour had mounted to his face. He looked as if he suddenly come to a conclusion. But Bertram answered the mediator firmly, for he was one of those simple characters who never desert their purpose, "I say I will fight, and save Vera from this incarnate devil. Come with me, Bentley, and I will thank you: leave me – and I will fight without you. But to leave this place without sending a bullet at that villain ... it is as far from me as flying."

Bentley bent his brows, and spoke slowly, "It is repugnant to me," he said, "not being a man of blood, to join these fool's fireworks: but I suppose that if you will go, you had better go with one sane man than without him. I will come."

"At 4 o'clock, I should think," said Bertram, calmly.

D'Avigdor nodded, and Bertram and his second moved out, leaving him brooding over the fire.

A wide and lonely field some miles from the town saw, at the stated hour, the advent of four men, of whom two were Lieutenant d'Avigdor, looking very pale and splendid, and a dubious-looking Italian officer whom he had brought with him. They soon greeted the appearance of Messrs. Bertram and Bentley, the former dark and chafing, the latter worried and scornful.

"Well, sir," said the Italian officer to Bentley, "unless any amicable arrangement can be arrived at..."

Bentley stood close to his principle's ear. "Now is your time," he said, *sotto voce*, "if you don't approve of being a murderer."

"I will fight," replied Bertram in a hard voice.

Similar appeals being made to d'Avigdor, he answered them with a quiet refusal: and the seconds measured the ground. Bertram took a pistol and stood facing his enemy. He must have known he had, ordinarily speaking, no chance, for d'Avigdor was a marksman and a duellist, and could bring him down easily with his shot. Bentley stood holding a handkerchief and ascertained they were ready.

Bertram saw the white handkerchief drop: fired blindly forward: and staggered a little back, dazed by the shock and smoke. When he looked for d'Avigdor he could not see him, for the seconds bending over him. He sent one horrible cry, like a man starting from a long dream, and hurled himself towards the fallen man. D'Avigdor had raised himself on his elbow, with a smile on his pale and lofty features and held out his hand feebly. "I dare say I deserved all I've got, Bertram," he said, good-naturedly, "and I have got enough," as he sank back.

Bertram knelt at his feet, shaking and sobbing with dreadful sounds and broken words of agony, and covered his face as the other held out his hand.

"Lie still," said Bentley authoratively, for he seemed to have a melancholy lack of patience and assistance for the usual ceremonies of repentant dying. "Keep your arm still, or how can I tie it up. You're no more dead than I am, I tell you. Hold that end of the scarf, monsieur. That's right. Now help me to carry him home. If I can collect all these fools' limbs and keep them intact for another meeting," he muttered, "I consider I shall have done my duty by the club. Thank God he's only struck in the arm."

And so meditating, the trio carried d'Avigdor into the city at a rapid pace, where he was soon quietly esconced in a bed at the hotel and medically assured that the wound was not serious. Probably his relief at the news was hardly greater than that of his opponent who came with a pale, sad face to visit him day after day, his anger and hatred gone with the bullet, and only a horrible dream between him and his old school associations.

"You cannot think," he said to him, as he sat by him, "how thankful I am, even though you live to see me ashamed." D'Avigdor groaned, "It would have been better for me to have died hard and game, like the brute that I am, than to wake and remember my folly. But I did my best."

"Your best?" said Bertram, pausing.

D'Avigdor laughed feebly and seemed to avoid the subject: but Bertram pressed him suspiciously. "How was it that you did not hit me. I did not even hear your bullet go by."

"Didn't you?" said the other, smiling.

"D'Avigdor, in the name of heaven what did you do?"

"Nothing."

"You never fired at me ?"

"Why should I? You see: if I got potted off, they could easily have elected a new member: with my dying prayer that it might not be Lewis Holing. But if I shot you – why what," and he looked at him with the inexplicable smile of old times, "What would become of the cutting book?"

"We must be going, Bertram," said Bentley, drawing him away, trembling under the shock of some huge abasement, "Good-bye, d'Avigdor, we will be here tomorrow."

"Bentley!" said d'Avigdor, "One word with you." Bentley turned back and came close to him.

"Bentley, somebody whom I have not, thank God, the face to name... her name would be a shock to Bertram too, now... will you take her home to her husband: she knows you are an honest man and will go with you."

Bentley wrung his hand and promised: he was averse to female philandering and given to embarrassment of the squire of dames, but he was too much of a gentleman to refuse to go with a woman anywhere: and he sought her out, courteously suggesting a return to England. Her reckless gaiety and satire were gone after her imperiousness: she was like ashes that pass through the fire, and remain ghastly and faded. She looked at him quite quietly and mildly and said, "I will go with you, Mr. Bentley," with a kind of weary relief. They started the next day and on the journey the helpless and blasé woman approached to enjoying the society of the good-tempered and strong-minded humorist, whom she really liked, as most other clever people did.

At Calais they fell in with Horace Beauchamp, a relation of the lady, who was ready to see her to London, and the lady parted from her protector with something more approaching intelligent preference than she had known for any human being, since she sent Vernède broken-spirited from the library fire.

As Bentley was pacing the market of Calais, wondering what hotel he should put up at, he started back on the edge of the quay, so as to nearly send him to a watery grave, or as he himself expressed it "to that great Hotel where Death carves and worms are the waiters": for just in front of him stood a small dark-haired, hazel-eyed lad with an olive complexion and a quiet suit, who came rapidly towards him.

"Father Abraham!" exclaimed Bentley, holding out his hand, "It is Lawrence!"

Chapter V. Nihilism

> Gehazi by the hue that pales thy cheek…
> And Pilate by the hue that stains thy hand though thou speak
> All Christ: with lips most murderous and most meek.
>
> ***Swinburne (The White Czar)***

We must now change the scene of our scattered and complicated drama to a room in St. Petersburg, where Gilbert Chesterton and his wife were sitting, or to speak more accurately, his wife was sitting and he was prowling up and down. On the table lay a letter from Sir Leonard Magnus, the new Member of Parliament for Bayswater, which they were discussing.

"Well," said the male species, pausing and striking his foot on the fender, "I don't see how I am to look after his people today, as I have the old soldiers' children as well as the Jews' Quarter to go and see: it must be managed, though, somehow..."

"Where do the people Magnus helps live?" asked the wife suddenly, raising her head on which the chestnut hair burnt like a red fire in the light of the embers. The husband named the place with some surprise.

"I can go to them," she said, rising quickly.

"You! No, thank God, you can't, while I'm here."

"Why not?" she cried, stamping her foot. "It must be done. I will go."

"But they are suspected."

She drew herself up, showing her tall figure, hidden generally in her strange coiled and crouching attitudes, and pushed back her flaming hair. "Do you think I am afraid?" she said.

"Do you think I am a sneaking brute?" he cried. "No... you are not afraid: I know you well, Gertrude, but by God's help wherever you go I go first: and..."

"And I'm a fool and can't do anything by myself," she cried excitedly, the flame of the passion of her strange girlhood rising for an instant to her eyes, "We are not to help you: we are to sit and be protected: a pretty office for a rational being in God's universe... where are your ideas of the mission and work of women; they lie in that street for me: or nowhere. I demand to do some useful work and take some honest risk. I am going."

"Gertrude," said the other, "it is better for us to walk by the highest thought, even though it slays us. You shall go..."

Gilbert Chesterton returned that night to the house he had been tenanting and found it silent. He called his wife's name twenty times and dashed hither and thither, filled with the tumult of thoughts that seemed to crowd round a fear he did not name. Leaving the house half topsy-turvy he searched the streets and squares, breathing hard and hoarsely. He could see no trace: and at last he threw himself against a wall, face to face with the fact that she must have been siezed by the government. For four hours he was insane. Then, when the light of reason began to struggle back into his brain, he hastened towards the nearest police centre, in the frantic hope that he might stop it yet. He came face to face, still white and panting, with a methodical-looking young officer, who waited civilly for him to speak coherently: then his words came, low and rasping: "Do you know anything of the kidnapping of a lady, Chesterton, by your men, five hours ago."

The officer looked down with a faint smile and was silent.

"Can you let me see her?" said the interrogator.

The officer looked out of the window as if no-one were speaking.

"Give me any statement of her charge and what is to be done... well, answer, please."

The officer looked round. "Her charge," he said, smiling, "whose charge?"

"This lady's: my wife," cried Chesterton, shaking with rage.

"We know nothing about it," said the official blandly.

"No such thing has occurred in our jurisdiction I assure you." Annoyed, he added with a faint sneer, "Nothing to do with us, you know … ha! … devil! … let me go, I say"

"You cur," hissed the other, pinning him by the throat and pressing him slowly back, "you accursèd slave and liar: tell the truth, or by the God whose arch-enemy you serve I will beat out your brains against the wall… I am thankful, in this babbling time, to have found one lying throat at my arm's end to preach a plain sermon to: … tell me the truth, I say."

The livid officer made a faint gasp as he bent back under the force: he had just strength to cry brokenly " … Help! … Lieutenant …" and tumbled back over the chair to the ground.

There was a noise within and a brown, good-natured-looking officer sprang into the room and laid a strong hand on the shoulder of the assaulter of justice: instead, however, of completing his purpose of forcing the rioter away from his victim, the reinforcement paused, stared, burst out laughing and sat down, remarking, not precisely in perfect, but indubitably in native English, that it was his intention to be blowed. Chesterton looked him in the face and beheld that it was the countenance of Langdon-Davies, in the uniform of a Russian police-officer. The next moment, while Chesterton was still staring, the laughter was subdued, and the officer rose to his feet again, helping his comrade to rise and retire. "You leave this ruffian to me," he said, reassuringly, "I'll have him dropped on for this, and for more besides after a little conversation."

The other laughed with weak ill-nature and disappeared, upon which the young English recruit executed a momentary war-dance, accompanied with the waving of fists, and then came back to the prisoner.

"Chesterton," he said, shaking his hand and laughing immoderately, "I am really delighted to see you – but, may I ask, what in the name of all the lobworms brings you here."

"I came after my wife: these hounds have taken her."

Langdon-Davies face grew serious. "You will hardly find that they will admit it," he said.

"God will help me," said his friend, very white and fierce, "even in this plot-benighted hell. I knew that tyranies had to outrage. I did not know how much they had to lie."

"Be quiet," said Langdon-Davies, abruptly rising, "You mustn't talk like that here." And he began to walk up and down the room, quick changes passing over his face. At last he stopped and fronted the prisoner, with a steady gaze.

"Confound it," he said with a smile, "Vieisti Galilei: The J.D.C. is too much for me ... Chesterton, hold your tongue: keep your opinions from your lips and your fingers from the regulation coat-collars, and I will do my best for you: in spite of this." And he hit himself on the facings of his uniform. "I will do my best to land you with your wife: the deuce knows where it will land me."

Chesterton broke in with frantic thanks.

"Thank you, Chesterton," he rejoined, "and now what am I to do: ... I know ... the first thing is to telegraph for our friends."

"What friends?" asked the other.

"I'm going to manage this," said Langdon-Davies and left the room.

That evening the prisoner and the somewhat

lenient officer of justice who was supposed to be keeping him in custody took tea together. Langdon-Davies was silent but seemed to be expecting something. Chesterton was gnawing out his heart in a fierce helplessness: when there came a knock on the outer door. Langdon-Davies sprang up to open it, and Chesterton, his brow darkening, snatched up a pistol.

Advancing cautiously to the door, he heard a voice he knew say, "There he is." He dropped the pistol with a great throb and stepped back, just as two figures came swiftly into the room, one the strong figure, and grave brows, of Bentley, and the other a slight, dark, grey-eyed companion, Lawrence Solomon. Chesterton took his friends' hands and almost broke down. Who should say that boy's companionships were vain or fleeting? He made them sit on each side of him, and forgot his misery for ten minutes. Then it came back to him like a cloud across the sun, and he told his wretched story in a few bitter words that vibrated like swords hacking the empty air.

"But if the Devil be not God," he cried out at the end, "I will fight my way to her, though I fight it alone."

"I hope you know," said Bentley after a long silence, "that you will not have to go alone."

Lawrence murmured in warm assent and Chesterton looked from one to the other and felt that his soul had come to the outpost and limit of language.

"Look here," struck in Langdon-Davies, "Listen to me and I will show you how to get there."

Two months afterwards a little band of travellers were progressing by means of a caravan, or rather in company with one, for all were frequently walking, across the great plain that stretched towards the East. Some way in front of the horses went Lawrence

Solomon, axe in hand, humming and whistling to himself along the pale deserts of snow. At the horses' heads was Bentley, swearing at them as protoplasms and blastoderms, and – and saying that he would see them damned first, together with other specimens of a scientific system of objurgation of his own invention. Chesterton was inside the caravan rummaging among the tools, rifles and provisions, while far at the rear of the procession hung Langdon-Davies, gun in hand, keeping watch for man or beast.

"I wish there were some animals to kill," he called out mournfully.

"I wish you'd come and kill these horses," said Bentley, " … Whoa, you Peribleu, you … they might go faster then. What a rattling pace we are going at. John was an undertaker compared to us."

"You don't want to kill the horses and have to leave them, do you?" said Chesterton from the interior of the waggon.

"I certainly don't want to kill them and have to carry them with me … Well, if I may parody a passage from the writing of the Rev. Charles Kingsley: I should remark Eastward Ho!"

Lawrence, who was out of earshot turned round. "I say, Chesterton," he called out, "this is rather jolly than otherwise."

"Yes," replied Bentley, "I have really only one wish to complete it: but there not being any piebald horses wandering about these neighbourhoods, or any glass windows provided to see the moon through, I leave them unuttered."

"What is the wish?" said Lawrence.

"I wish Maurice was here," replied the other.

"Wherever he is," said Chesterton speaking for the first

time, "he will think of us, as we of him. We have found friends very true to us so far and we need not doubt."

Bentley said something, and far ahead rose the clear voice of Lawrence ringing over the desolate Caucasian plain:

"In the neighbourhood of Kensington where the bird
sings on the tree
Live the members of a society, which is called the J.D.C."

Once again in that lonely place four voices took up the chorus of Bentley's old song:

"I'm a member, I'm a member, member of the J.D.C.
I belong to it for ever: don't you wish that you were me."

And chaunting aloud, the cortège moved into the pathless wastes.

Chapter VI. The dangers of the sea

"Ye winds that have measured your sport,
Convey to this desolate shore
Some cordial end… report
Of the land I shall visit no more."

Cowper

On the sunshiny deck of an Australian liner, scudding through blazing wastes of summer sea, two passengers were lounging, who presented a strong contrast in their appearance. One was a tall, stalwart fresh-coloured man with a deprecating manner, a prominent commercial and political figure recently knighted as Sir Hubert Sams. The other was a small dark lad, with curly black hair and large grey eyes. He was a rising mathematician, but he never protruded his speciality in conversation, being able and pleased to talk of other things. His name was Maurice Solomon.

"Well," said Sams at length, "I am sure I came away from the club feeling the Chairman's prophecies very much, but I hardly thought to meet a Debater so unexpectedly ... Oh, let me introduce you. Mr. Maurice Solomon – Mrs. Peile. Miss Dorothy Grey – Mr. Maurice Solomon."

Mr. Maurice Solomon bowed and greeted the ladies with some interest for a letter or two from Bentley and Vernède had made him acquainted with the name of Vera Peile, the brilliant and imperial woman who stood before him now, a ghostly and woe-stricken figure in widow's weeds, for General Peile was dead. She had been almost dying, when Sir Hubert Sams had agreed to take her upon a voyage, which had ensured her recovery: and now she moved about weakly and drearily, seeming to care for nothing save the society of Dorothy, Bentley's generous and sensible cousin, who shared the usefulness, as well as the humour of her kinsman.

When Dorothy heard the stranger's name, she smiled and seemed interested. "I have often heard my cousin Edmund talk about you, Mr. Solomon," she said, "In fact, at one time he used to talk about nothing else."

Maurice laughed but seemed touched and pleased. "Did he warn you to look after the spoons?" he enquired.

"No," answered the girl, laughing, "That would have been too delicate a subject. He never talked shop."

Whereupon they both laughed hilariously, when their conversation was interrupted more decisively than by any words, by a weary look upon the face of the invalide. Sir Hubert, with immense ceremony, offered his arm to Vera, while Maurice followed behind with her companion.

At the cabin door when the ladies disappeared, Sir Hubert also said good night, and Maurice Solomon came back alone onto the lonely star-lit deck. Leaning over the bulwarks, he watched the moon struggling up through fierce rifts behind the low craggy coral-reefs of one of the little Pacific islands not more than 100 yards away. He grew tired of his position, and being extremely active, he slung himself like a monkey onto the edge of the bulwarks, hanging on by a shroud and gazing dreamily at the island. Suddenly, just by his ear there was a sound of a rope snapped, and then the noise of fighting water in his ears. He rose twice from the roaring ocean darkness, before he could clear his eyes and begin to swim. Already the ship, where no-one had seen him fall overboard, was almost out of sight. He sent one hopeless and useless shout after it, and then by blind instinct and the habit of a good swimmer struck out for the island. After a few minutes swimming and a brief struggle in the surf, he crawled dazed and dripping up the slope of the unknown sands, and looked around him.

Certainly, if it was fated that one of the members of the Junior Debating Club was to be cast on a desert island, there could not have been a better choice than Maurice Solomon, except perhaps Bentley, in the matter of readiness and resource. His quietness, intelligence and serious ideas gave many people the impression of his being like his brother pre-eminently a studious fellow, but the truth was that the real powers of the young mathematician lay much more in the practical and industrial region. He had picked up in his friendship with Bentley a fair knowledge of science; he had passed his time at home in endless industry at mending watches, working out riders, taking photographs and managing little theatres, his health was good, his courage considerable and his temper happy... but at the moment of which we write, his clothes very wet. He pulled some of them off and hung them on thickets to dry, and when the flaming sun had rapidly accomplished that object he put them on and looked aroud him again. He heard distinctly the sound of running water some way off and followed the sound.

A few minutes walking brought him to a cleft or ravine in the heart of which shone the stream, half-hidden in thickets, grotesque cactus and stumpy and knotted palms, among which sounded every now and then the hoarse cry of a hornbill. Having refreshed his thirst with the water of the brook, and partaken of some wild fruit, which his speciality of botanical knowledge enabled him to identify, he looked round for some greater facilities for spending the night. He saw struggling over the stream a little higher up, a large tree of the branched and leafy order, which appeared to offer the greatest possible facilities for taking up permanent quarters. He lost no time in scrambling up to the top and found that the space between the radiating branches was a flat space of some four yards square....

Chapter VII. The Robber of the Mountains

> And Kamal has taken him by the hand and set upon his feet.
> "No talk shall be of dogs," he said, "When wolf and grey wolf meet.
> May I eat dirt if thou hast hurt of me in deed or breath.
> What mother of lances brought thee forth to jest at the dawn
> with death?"
>
> ***Rudyard Kipling***

Night was drawing rapidly towards twilight in a ravine

in the south of Siberia, down which were quickly but cautiously riding a knot of armed horsemen, with a lady in their midst. Suddenly the silence, disturbed only by the muffled trot of the horse, was broken sharply by a sound like the breaking of a twig upon the slope. One of the horsemen wheeled round and said something in a loud, hoarse whisper, and the cavalcade stopped. The rider in question, whose broad-brimmed hat and cartridge belt did not hide the severe features and eyeglasses of Bentley, moved on himself to a lower position, whence he saw on the dark slopes above a sudden spark blurred the next moment with smoke and followed by a reverberation among the hills. Bentley unslung his carbine and turned to his companions. "Come on: gallop!" he shouted, and then levelling his barrel he sent a bullet at their assaillants and flew down the gorge. His friends came thundering behind and leaving the first detachment of Russian Police behind met the second body in full career. Langdon-Davies sent two bullets point blank through the body of one man and, knocking over another with the butt, was disarmed by a third, whom he was just prepared to close with, when the man was flung from his horse by Lawrence. Langdon-Davies got hold of his sabre and fell to fighting again. Meanwhile three horsemen had made a desperate dash at the prisoner, who was of course Gertrude, but Chesterton had brained one of them, and a bullet, coming no-one knew whence, had struck the other in the hip, so that he reeled and tumbled from his horse. The last of the policemen made one last rush and was beaten down by Bentley, who, breaking through the reeling remnants of the enemy, led the fugitives, whirling like the wind, down the mountains, leaving pursuit far behind.

A week's riding among the Mongolian and Afghan villages brought the fugitive rescue-party to the foot of the Himalayas, beyond which mysterious rampart they knew that they would be safe. They had not, however, gone two or three days march up the lower passes before they met with another cause for alarm. Lawrence who was, as was the custom on the march, riding ahead reined up, and turning to the rest, intimated that there was some danger. Scarcely had the words left his lips than he had to grasp his gun and level at the turbanned heads of two weird-looking Sikhs, who knife in hand started from the bushes at his horse's head. Before the rest could come up, some nine or ten more Indians emerged from the bushes and crowded grinning towards Lawrence, who did not budge.

"Repugnant as it is to my feelings," said Bentley, calmly, as he rode up, "a stern sense of duty demands that I should remark – a rescue ho!" With which words, being a young man of considerable strength, he knocked both of the Sikhs down. A third, spear in hand, made a dash at him, but dropped with Lawrence's bullet in his shoulder: and Langdon-Davies and Chesterton having come up, the Sikhs paused rather and looked about them. The other party following their example, they perceived that their foes were reinforced by a picturesque cohort of lancers with orange turbans and black horses, who came slowly down the ravine with gleaming eyes fixed on the intruders. When this desperate-looking train had gathered in motley but artistic groups behind their erratic infantry, they revealed behind them a still more princely staff of Indian warriors, whose bronzed faces contrasted strangely with their resplendant silver-embossed shields and flashing steel breast-plates, and in the ring of this last guard of honour rose a tall, wild figure, whose dark and haggard, though not asiatic, face was over-shadowed by a jewelled turban surmounted by a fiery red plume. His sash was stuck full of silver-mounted knives, and the abject hommage with which he was treated by all his followers showed the religious reverence to a prophet mingled with the natural subordination to a bandit chief. Nearer and nearer came the mountain brigand, his subjects making way for him, to the pale, but resolute group of wanderers. When he came close to them, he raised his dark eyes and thin face and, after a moment's gaze, a wild fire sprang into his eyes. At the same moment Chesterton was seen to shake with some sudden emotion, and Lawrence uttered a sharp cry. It was echoed in a loud shout from Langdon-Davies, and Bentley moved quietly forward. "How are you, Oldershaw?" he said, and held out his hand. The outlaw caught it and bowed speechless over his saddle bow, and the next moment the three others were close to him clinging to his hand and arm and struggling with their voices.

"Lucien," said Chesterton at last, in difficult accent, "Lucien, you are here: what does it mean?"

"Oh, I don't know: it is a long story," said Oldershaw with a trembling lip: "Lawrence... Langdon... come all of you to the camp and I will tell you everything..."

"My children," he said in Hindustannee, turning to his wondering tribe, who turned a sea of faces up to him, "these are my brothers. Even the four stars of the west: adore them. Let them go before you ever as gods, unto the tent of the prophet of the gods.

BASIL HOWE,
A STORY OF YOUNG LOVE

Book One

Chapter 1

A Spectator & A Drama

A long, sunburnt, angular young man, somewhat young for the black frock coat and solemn tall hat he wore, but without a bright touch of dandyism was leaning over the grey stone bulwarks of a seaside parade above a ragged bit of German ocean. His eyes were not however riveted upon the changes of the breakers but upon the various phases, the goings and comings, the motley and humorous groups of human beings below. These he regarded with a wistful gaze that suggested the most melancholy of men. He had for some time been the quiet observer of one incident, which introduces us to the subject of our story. And this is what he saw. On a steep and loose yellow sand were sitting or rather lying, two fervid, square-faced, particularly English looking girls, in white summer frocks and with the clear lines of happiness, honesty, education, on their full frank features.

The elder of them, whose face was paler, and her brow and chin more resolute than the others, was engaged in some serious and business-like discussion, not untinged with irritation, to which the other's contributions were more intermittent. Any one acquainted with the ways of large families might have guessed from the very tone of their voices that they could be speaking of nothing but a younger sister. Even if the unconscious (or very possibly conscious) subject of their complaints had not been standing within three feet of them, a lithe, long-legged girl of fourteen, with a tempest of red hair blown across her by the sea-wind. She had the same open features but there was a more defiant look in them, and her lips fell in a half contemptuous fullness. "I think Margaret," said the eldest girl to her companion, whose head was dropped into a book "you might tell me a little of what you think about it, when you know I'm doing my best." Margaret looked up with a lazy admiration in her grey eyes: "I know you are dear," she said good-temperedly; "but what's the good of asking me? About Gertrude I think just as you do; I don't like her raging herself into tears, or laughing herself into hysterics; it's not sensible. I don't like her new airs, nor her vanity, nor her friend Cécile Fleury, who is a fool. But if you can't manage her, there's not much chance of my doing it. You were created to manage people and do things all for people's own good. I was created to read this book, or at least I'm going to. Let me alone, dear." And she went on with her reading. The elder went on speaking, thoughtfully, as if in a brown study. "You see, it is not merely her doing just as she likes and taking up with Cécile, who is certainly not a nice girl. I wish we didn't have to know her: all that can be stopped and shall be. But her fits of violence are so sudden and fearful I sometimes dream she will really go mad. In her worst time I have seen her roll over and over on the floor, shrieking: most people in the house were frightened of her, but I do not get frightened of things, somehow. But the question is… Now look there!… Gertrude! Gertrude, come down from that!" The resolute elder had sprung to her feet and was excitedly calling to her rambling youngest sister who, to her horror, had climbed to a ledge of the flint-built breakwater of the harbour and was capering along it, past the point where the breakers flooded its base. Above her rose the smooth face of the wall to the rampart above, below it fell to the hoarse foam of the sea, and along the perilous footway the daring girl was moving to a point overhanging deep and whirling water. She did not feel quite comfortable, courageous as she was, but just as she was minded to return, she heard her sister's loud and clear voice imperatively demanding retreat. Her prompt answer was a wild, almost fiend-like laugh and an immediate bound to a yet more dizzy position.

"Everybody is looking at you," vociferated her sister Catherine, with a characteristically inventive appeal to her sister's self-love. The wanderer's answer was lost in the crash of a wave, but it is much to be feared that her reply to her sister was something to the effect that it was more than could be said of her. When the reckless girl had reached the extreme possible point and was calmly wetting her feet on the shining stones and the soaking sea-weed, she happened to look mockingly over her shoulder, and saw that in the meantime the tide had risen and was practically at that moment cutting off her retreat. Her sister again called to her to return in maddened, but not less varied and plausible appeals.

Just as Gertrude was standing, shaking with the conflict of scorn and fear, she heard a grave voice above her say, in a deeply apologetic tone, "Excuse me, but if you are superstitious about drowning, you had better come upstairs." This somewhat mystifying sentence was delivered in a melancholy tone that masked its intricate humour for a moment, and Gertrude, on looking up, beheld leaning over the rampart of the flat perpendicular wall above her, the brown, hawk-like face and black elbows of the young man before mentioned. Laughing in spite of her perplexity at the proposal to come upstairs, she asked how the manoeuvre was to be effected. "Oh," he replied, gravely. "We might make an appointment to meet half-way. I shall be there all right." Here the sombre and conventional youth, by an incredibly sudden movement, brought his long legs clean over the bulwark and was seen hanging in air, with one hand clutching the edge and one foot poised on a slight foothold. "Hem, may I have a dance?" he said, holding out his hand. The girl, choking with laughter, caught hold, and by a quick leap and swing he set her safely upon the parade above thronged with people. Having regained his place, he made some darkly eccentric remark, and fell again into his unobtrusive attitude, a model of dry and deferential respectability.

But at this moment the two other sisters came up and he raised his hat slightly and dropped into the background. If Gertrude thought (as is indeed improbable) that in accepting the aid of the stranger she had done something risqué and offensive to her sisters, she was much mistaken. They thought nothing of it, beyond being pleased and amused, simply because they were sensible and natural children: for children they were in many respects, though both over seventeen. It is the advantage or disadvantage of good bringing up.

"We have to thank you for helping Gertrude," said Catherine cordially. "It was very kind of you to trouble."

"Ah… I am rather a great and good man, I know," he answered sadly. "The herd, however, do not know me. But it is getting near dinner time, so I must get home to tea. Greencroft Square has wandered a good way off by this time."

The first sister stopped in a laugh at his paradoxical sentences, and looked quickly at him. "You know Greencroft Square?" she said.

"We have a bowing acquaintance," he replied calmly. "Some relation of mine, I believe, once stayed there. He was, indeed, one whom I long retained in the capacity of father, an office which I found by experience, absolutely necessary to my existence. He has left it for some time now; I have it all to myself, except indeed for a kind of cousin, whom I occasionally find on the stairs, and to whom, I am told, the house now belongs." Margaret, still laughing and puzzled, scanned the dark, strangely marked features of the stranger, and asked him on what side of the square he lived. "Oh, on the inside," he replied wearily. "The name of my cousins, as I extorted from them in strict confidence, is Fleury."

"Fleury!" said Gertrude quickly, flushing with pleasure, "Then you know Cécile."

Catherine, though much too well bred to rebuke her sister in company, could not help stirring and biting her lip at the name of the obnoxious friend, who was really a flighty, morbid coquette enough. Gertrude turned to her, with defiant fire in her eyes. "I am glad we have discovered a cousin of Cécile's. She is my friend. Yes, my dear, depend upon it: I shall go and see her to-morrow. We live next door to her." And throwing up her head and her flaming locks over her shoulder, she walked away, rapidly followed by her grumbling sisters.

Chapter 2

The History of Three Babies

The family of Grey, to three of whom the reader was introduced in the last chapter, was emphatically a well brought-up family. That is to say they were not kicked up, or hustled up, neither did they fall up, an acrobatic feat performed by a large number of modern educated children, who have a nodding acquaintance with their parents. Good bringing up is the very opposite of mere severity, indeed when you hear of one of those solitary, severe fathers, who occur from time to time, you may infer certainly that he neglects his children and in all probability that he drinks. Good bringing up is the inducing of children to fall naturally and happily into certain rational rules and domestic traditions, so that they grow up with a healthy and honest childhood really built up and completed as part of their characters. With nine children out of ten, this system, or rather atmosphere of practical good government works well, but there is a minority, people of a certain type, with whom it does not work, and for whom something more is required. This may be said to be the problem of this book.

It may be noticed that an author generally writes from inside one of his characters, and outside the others. He analyses the history and looks with the eyes of one set of characters, while the others, perhaps more important, he builds up, like a spectator from indications and discoveries. The tall, subdued young man who was an onlooker and participator in the scene which we took as typical of the relations of the three sisters, was a shrewd and keen-eyed character, but he would have been better able to really grasp those relations, if he had had the privilege, as the reader has, of hearing a little of their history, and having a glimpse of their earlier childhood. He was, however, then far away, an odd, active, thoughtful little tadpole at a public school: and he only met a family that were destined to have no little influence on his life, when their characters were to some extent formed.

Those unintelligent, and, we should venture to say, certainly unmarried philosophers who say that new-born infants are "blank sheets of paper", possessing no natural cast of mind, would have received six severe counter-arguments, had they been present, in the three pairs of eyes, of three particular babies, as they sat in a line against the nursery wall. Catherine, the eldest child, was then five years old, round, swarthy and Japanese, still free from the pallor which afterwards resulted from ceaseless household and social activity by night and day. She was a rotund, solemn baby, even then suggesting by her neat frock, bound up hair and demure manner, the character of a small housekeeper that always clung to her. She was always the governing and systematising spirit in the nursery pastimes, often to the displeasure of her companions: she had, however, decidedly a temper of her own, and a stamp of her small foot and the sudden clenching of her small hands generally promised the attainment of her own way. With this dash of temper, she was, however, emphatically a good girl, fearless, truthful, utterly imbued with the unselfishness which is of so weighty a value in a family of children. All these qualities may have as yet appeared only by indications at the time we speak of, but they all looked out, with a thoughtfulness, not dreamy but resolute, in those round, dark, blinking eyes.

Margaret, the second child, was only a few months younger. She was even rounder than her sister, had china-blue eyes and a smile of such utter and eternal contentment as reminded one of a Buddhist in the Nirvâna. It never left her features under any circumstances, nor could anyone ever discover what was the source of her perennial satisfaction. That she was inimitably good-natured, and that she had a habit of saying innocently humorous things after long silences of contemplation, was as much as had yet been discovered with regard to her character.

Nature, which had left all the heat and pride of the first character entirely out of Margaret, seemed to have made up by compounding the third child's personality, to all appearance, entirely out of those materials. It is conjectured that of the first year or two of her existence, she roared very much the larger part: in fact the impression of the visitor was that she was made with her mouth open and a legion of fiends inside. As, however, both the other girls had gone through minor forms of this frenzy, the child was sensibly and good-temperedly dealt with, and brought through the clamorous first years, with plenty of remaining health and energy. It was soon found, however, that she was emphatically a tartar. All kinds of phases, severally lawless and peculiar, passed over her character. At one time she was an absolute wild cat, ready to fly at those who provoked her, to yell and struggle and bite, as if for life: and though this stormy period passed, it left a part of her nature, which, sometimes in rare moments, looked out of her large eyes. Her eyes, even as a child, were peculiar. They were not a clear blue like Margaret's, nor a deep blue-black, like Catherine's: but appeared to be a kind of grey-green that was sometimes a sleepy blue-grey and sometimes a fierce, pale green: changing to these and myriad other shades at different moods and moments. At another time she had a furious passion for mischief, especially for hiding keys, locking doors, and other paltry practical jokes: and in time this passed also. Then came an insane habit of running away and losing herself. Four times she was hunted and recaptured, once in the London streets and three times over the bare hills in the country, always her favourite playground. Her sisters who, owing to her mother's literary occupations, had almost entire charge, ranted and reasoned in vain. There seemed to be no rational vein in her, no sense of order or insight into necessities to which to appeal. At the age of thirteen Gertrude was a reckless, scornful tomboy, with raw red hair and a high-pitched voice. About this time a fourth phase appeared, in some respects the most ominous of all. She became absolutely silent, listless and dull. Her life from one year's end to the other was a protracted sulk: shrewd people were positively frightened at the change, and wondered what would become of the high spirit which was so perilously sealed up. During this solitary brooding time, an evil time for any child, she began to be seen about the company of Cécile Fleury, a handsome, silly French schoolgirl, whose presence, slight as it seemed, marked a great and dreadful change. How it came, no one knew: the tale of that misanthropic silence was never told, but sure it is that Gertrude Grey had fallen from the Eden of the well-kept household, with its spontaneous contentment and its mild austerity, and had become – a silly schoolgirl. She had eaten of the gaudy apple, and had become as Cécile, knowing good and evil.

Spiritual sympathy might have averted this, but spiritual sympathy is no part of ordinary good bringing up even at its best.

Chapter 3

An Introduction

Through the large, lovely, dusty drawing-room of the Fleury's house in Greencroft Square, the typical house of a broken down aristocratic family, two young girls were wandering, twined in that peculiarly unmeaning embrace peculiar to girls' younger friendships, the fiery aureole of Gertrude close to the long black curls of her friend Cécile. Why they adopted this attitude, it is not easy to explain for, though they were constant and talkative companions, Gertrude did not love her friend in any emotional sense of the word, and Cécile was rather contemptuous and, at the same time, rather frightened of Gertrude. We will not inflict on the reader the whole of Miss Fleury's conversation: for indeed Gertrude gathered only scraps of it. She had a habit of falling into sudden fits of abstraction, almost like trances, and picking up fragments of a conversation. Cécile appeared to be speaking of a gentleman, a friend of her brother's, and he hardly interested Gertrude. Sensitive vanity, and a pleasure in the intoxication of *general* applause, were the worst forms of frivolity that had damaged her naturally healthy nature. "He is very entertaining," she said, "and unlike other people: he never pays one compliments, but says odd sentences that you can't make head or tail of. You should see him, dear. I will introduce you. He has dark hair, and hard blue eyes that are always the same. He is very neatly dressed, but never seems to remember he has clothes on, somehow. Why, dear me, I believe he is out in the garden now.” Gertrude, as we say, had only heard odds and ends of the lengthy description, but the last sentence awakened her curiosity, always a rampant passion in her character, and she said, promptly: “Let’s go and look at him, then.”

“Oh no, no!” said Cécile, hastily, and with many asseverations of denial, which the more simple-minded Gertrude was quite at a loss to comprehend. Gertrude, however, when roused, was the more decided character of the two, and without honouring her friend with another word, ducked past her and took flying leaps down the steps into the garden. Then she stopped dead, and felt angry and mortified. For just in front of her was seated on an old log, reading, the lean, lithe, almost snake-like figure and long dark head of her chance acquaintance of the shore, whom she now remembered having described himself as a cousin of the family.

She stood chafing, with feelings it is difficult to analyse: somehow the atmosphere of Cécile did not seem to harmonise with her views of her stiff, quaint fellow-guest. The latter was on his feet in a moment, with a rapid salutation, and Cécile, who had come up at this moment and who could look really graceful and queenly when she liked, introduced him as Mr. Basil Howe. “I have met Mr. Howe before, as it happens,” said Gertrude, with a smile of gruesome reminiscence.

“You have indeed met me before,” said Howe, seriously, “and I trust you are quite recovered.”

“Oh yes,” replied Gertrude, laughing. “I hope we shall see something of you in the future.”

“You may see something of me,” said Howe dryly, “almost all of me in fact. I hope to show myself in a more amiable light than when I enacted the part of the proverbial gentleman, between whom and the deep blue sea your choice was so rapidly made. But I hope I am not keeping you from any important discussion," he added hastily. "I myself am so lazy I have hardly time to do anything. Would you like to walk round the garden: the snails are coming out beautifully this year. How much we may learn from their activity and intelligence! You prefer flowers, I think, Miss Fleury."

"I adore flowers," said Cécile languidly, and fool as she was, she really did.

"I frequently adore them myself," he replied, "but here, if my eyes do not deceive me (and they are the most faithful set I ever had) come Miss Grey's sisters, together with a necktie, behind which I have no difficulty in discerning my cousin Lucien."

A thin wasted young man, in a smart Parisian cravat and light grey suit: with regular features, watery eyes and a ghastly grin, moved up and offered two kid fingers to Gertrude and to Howe, which were received in the first case with a childish shyness still strong in her nature, and in the second with a grave cordiality always noticeable in his. To no-one, neither to Cécile nor Lucien, in their most irritating phases, did he ever lose his austere good-humour. Catherine and Margaret came up at this moment, in company with an aunt, a slight, stately lady of sixty, with a curious crown of grey frizzled hair, and all were presented to the darkly deferential stranger.

"The fact is," Catherine was saying to Howe, "we were planning some kind of picnic expedition up the river to Dartwood Deep, at which," she added, impelled by natural generosity as much as civility, "we should be very pleased to see you join us. You know Dartwood Deep, Mr. Howe?"

"It was the home of my childhood," he replied promptly, "the scene of my happiest married years. Where is Dartwood Deep?"

"About three miles up the river," replied Catherine smiling. "We have been there before."

"I have never been there before," replied Howe, gazing at the distance, "but I should have the very greatest pleasure in going there again. It is really very kind of you to ask me at all, particularly as I can't invite you to a picnic in my own house. However, if you will tell me what day you are going, I might happen to choose that day myself."

"Well," said Catherine in her rapid business tones, "we thought of the day after tomorrow. The river will be clear after the Bank Holiday. Not tomorrow because Gertrude has a singing lesson;... yes, Gertrude, you must go to your singing lesson... I wish you wouldn't say 'Shan't', Gertrude... and then you see everyone will be free on Saturday. Could you be at our house at 10, Mr. Howe?"

"Certainly, Miss Grey," was the reply.

It is characteristic of Gertrude that the trifling rebuke of her hurried sister had waked within her all the unquenchable and inexplicable passions that had made her childhood that of a literal maniac: and she watched fiercely for her moment of revenge.

"Of course," she said, with an impudent smile, "of course Cécile goes with us in the boat."

Catherine's clear brow clouded, but she looked her sister full in the face. "Of course," she said imperiously.

"Oh how nice! You must be pleased," cried Gertrude, all her eyes and teeth lightening maliciously. Catherine, who was not without a spark of the same fire buried severely under her iron will, her social versatility, and her devouring conscientiousness, turned sharply away and spoke to Howe, "I think we must get home now: remember the time is 10 o'clock. Good morning."

"Good morning, as you suggest," he replied. "I am afraid I have been keeping you from all sorts of things you didn't want to do. I myself have got to go and finish lying on the grass. Good morning."

And hastily raising the big black hat, the stranger took great strides away over the lawn, the rest moving off in another direction. Before, however, they were out of sight, Howe, a mark of whose solitary social impartiality it was that he never sought a second interview with any of the people he treated with such good-tempered formality, gave one rapid glance backwards at the group he was leaving. His eyes rested for a moment, with a shrewd, puzzled look, on a slight, straight girlish figure, crowned with great plumes of red hair, who followed her bustling family in sullen solitude.

Chapter 4

Some Mixtures and an Explosion

Into the gleaming shallows, chequered with shadows of elm and willow, of the river below Dartwood, a rowing-boat, laden with a happy-looking company, was pushing ashore. In the stern seats were four ladies, one old and three young, of whom two, with fair hair, were sisters, and one with dark hair, a stranger. A third sister was rowing stroke in company with a pale, smiling young man dressed entirely in white, while a gaunt, bronzed high-featured stranger, still in his serviceable suit of black, was displaying great skill in bringing the boat to shore. As they drifted within some five feet of the shore, the dark, upright figure took a sudden and wholly miraculous leap alighting on the bank and hauling a rope after him.

"The best way to keep a boat still, I always find," he observed scientifically, "is to tie a shore to it. It will stand quite quiet then. Can I help you out, Miss Grey?"

Catherine and her sisters, however, sprang on shore without any difficulty, but Miss Cécile Fleury required all the support in the world before she could be languidly and gracefully disposed on the shore.

"I always find it so difficult to get on land," she said suavely to Howe.

"So do I," he answered, a reply that sprang from his universal habit of agreeing with everybody, but which contrasted somewhat humorously with his recent escapade. "It is much easier to get into the water if you prefer it. Where are we to go now, Miss Grey? Our lives and liberties are, as it were, in your hand. Give us the word."

"Well, I think," said Catherine, readily assuming the responsibility that Howe had good-naturedly attached to her, "I think perhaps we had better go first to the Abbey: there's a saint's tomb and some carvings there: and then come back here and have lunch."

"The same thing occurred to me," replied Howe readily, "after you had suggested it. I've been a saint myself in my time," a mysterious remark that provoked some laughter, "and there was always a grave at people's service if they would only call before lunch. Let us make haste and get to the tomb then, and have some fun. Are there any bones, Miss Grey?"

"I'm afraid not," said Catherine, laughing.

"Oh, I wish I'd known that," he answered, with regret. "I'd have had him measured for some. I'm using mine now, you see."

And he fell back unobtrusively to speak to Margaret. All his new acquaintances were disposed to an amused liking for the curious young man, but Gertrude, whose conscious tendency to analysis was stronger than her sisters', began to fit in the fragmentary indications of his character with a certain mystified interest. One thing she began to see: that dryly as he spoke and sombre as was his usual expression, he was by no means silent and the very reverse of unsociable. He liked to have companions, to talk to them by the yard in his own fantastic way: almost the only words she had ever heard from him, in which there was a thread of serious opinion, were when he said, "I don't believe in Great Silent Men myself. If a man has really anything to say, anything new or important or amusing, it's his natural instinct – to get rid of it as soon as possible." All through that walk to the abbey he was filling the ears of various groups of the party with the topsy-turvy utterances, most of them such as would look meaningless on paper, but filled with the quality that compels a sudden sense of the ludicrous the moment they are presented. As his ceaseless and impartial attention had a great effect on the drama that followed, we may take them briefly in scenes.

Howe (falling abreast of Margaret): Do you know this place of final, I may say, universal entertainment we are going to, Miss Grey?

Margaret: Oh yes... we often go there... (laughs) but we generally lose our way all the same.

Howe: Ah, yes. I thought you must sometimes take your little porringers and eat your suppers there. Is there a cicerone at the abbey? If you would do me a favour now... I wish, if you notice me inadvertently murdering him (I often do it to cicerones without thinking), I wish you would just draw my attention, you know, or remind me somehow. If I should do him any serious injury on the saint's premises, you might ask him to the picnic: not the saint, I mean – he is gone to that Great Picnic at which no hamper is necessary – but the cicerone. Do this, and I shall bless you whenever I remember to.

Margaret (with idle enjoyment of nonsense): Well, don't begin now: blessings are always so long-winded. And as for asking a cicerone to lunch... just think of hearing all about the window put here by the present duke, and the hat-peg put there by the former duke, when you want to do nothing but eat oranges. You remind me of Sir Roger de Coverly.

Howe: My family saw an early resemblance. But you cannot deceive me (which is a quotation). I know the passage to which you refer in the remarks of one whom no inclination but a stern sense of duty induces me to refer to as the "worthy knight". (Here Howe proceeds to repeat, at great length, the passage in *The Spectator* referred to, to the delight of Margaret, who reads everything and delights in Addison.)

Margaret (smiling): You have a splendid memory, Mr. Howe.

Howe (recklessly): Yes, it is rather a nice one, isn't it. I've had him several years now. (Looking round.) Excuse me, Miss Grey, for what might seem a reference to some connections of yours; but look at your youngest sister. What is the matter with her?

Margaret (smiling wearily, but with a blink like the flick of a lazy conscience): Ah, that is what we none of us know, Mr. Howe.

At this point Gertrude came bounding past them like a wild thing. Wind and the sight of fresh earth and foliage always acted as an intoxicant upon her, and as she came reeling by, with loose wildflowers in her hands and loose light hair, she looked half like a hamadryad inspired. When she saw Howe, she felt checked the slightest touch and hung, gazing. He stepped to her side as calmly as if she looked like a person possessed of the ordinary number of wits. A strange enough conversation took place as follows:

Howe: Would you mind my looking at that red flower a moment, Miss Grey? (She hands it to him in silence.) Thank you. The fact is I am thinking of having a waistcoat of the same colour and pattern. The idea is chaste, I think. That is a fine spray of Milkmaid's Bonnet-strings you have there.

Gertrude (who has begun to understand his tones and phrases, and something in his voice makes her say, with a curious smile): I don't believe that is its name at all.

Howe (in an injured tone): Don't you? No more do I. But it is wonderful what poetical names the country people give the flowers. Look at that hedge of Wild Bigamy there, and the Curates' Catapults that line our English lanes. I assure you I know the names of every flower and egg, just like the boy at the beginning of the book.

Gertrude (feeling a vague kind of gratitude for his companionable lunacy): Well, then what is that flower under the stone there?

Howe: Oh that – that is called Blue Jerusalem and is supposed to make clergymen dance when they see it. *Salem Geruleus* is the scientific name. But here we are at the grave we propose to put up at. Can you show me the carvings?

Gertrude (completely sobered and readily): Oh yes. They are round the other side.

"What a beautiful place this is," she added as she glanced up at the arches of the half-ruined abbey.

"It is a cosy little place," he replied, "and here are the carvings and my cousin Cécile."

"Is it not divine?" said that lady from a long way off, as they moved up.

"I thought it was a little divine, too," he answered, raising his eyebrows. "Why, I am convinced you might walk from one end of the Harrow Road to the other and not see anything like this. Nothing in the least approaching to it."

Cécile looked rather puzzled, and Gertrude tumbled over a half-laugh, as they drew up to the principal carving, a relief of St. Stephen undergoing martyrdom in the gauntest mediaeval spirit.

"Isn't it beautiful?" said Cécile, in an awe-struck voice.

"No," replied Gertrude, abruptly.

"That sweet carving not beautiful... Gertrude!" said Cécile hotly.

"I don't see anything beautiful about it," said Gertrude with bullet-headed honesty. "I don't see why St. Stephen should be so hideously starved and ugly, or why he should stand on one leg, with his head on one side, to be martyred. It isn't like people are, it isn't like people ought to be: why should I be made to like it? Why do you like it, Cécile?"

Cécile's handsome face clouded. She bit her lip to repress the sudden intuition that she didn't like it at all, felt angry with her friend and herself and said sharply: "I should like to know what Mr. Howe thinks."

Howe stood regarding the relief for some time in earnest scrutiny, and then began: "Well, I'm a bit of a protomartyr myself –" and he was cut short by a sharp ringing laugh from Gertrude, for his absolutely unmeaning but somehow irresistibly risible remark had given her a momentary victory over the sentimental anticipations of the imperious Cécile. Cécile, however, who was by no means a fool, made her point instantly:

"I wish you would let Mr. Howe finish his sentence. Gertrude," she said.

"I wish she would help me to finish them," said Howe, coming to her rescue at a bound. "She might perhaps weave into them a golden thread of sanity which is not usually observable. As for our host," he said, glancing for a second at the stone-battered saint, but seeming to have all his eyes on the temporary sullenness of Cécile, "and the religious disabilities under which he is represented as labouring, I am bound to say that I think the carving very good, a statement I make with the authority proper to one who knows nothing whatever about it: and I am very much obliged to you all for bringing me here."

The statement was fenced round with all his characteristic wish to please everybody, but Cécile had her victory. She took advantage of a momentary withdrawal of Howe to take orders from Catherine to say to Gertrude, "Mr. Howe seems to understand these artistic matters very well." The remark was innocent, but there was a flicker of spitefulness on her lips, and Gertrude knew well the meaning. "All right," she broke out stormily, "if Mr. Howe is so wondrously clever, go and talk to him, instead of me. I'm a fool. I can't understand it; no, I can't, and I think it ugly. Go on. Only remember this, no stranger would ever have made me speak to you as you've spoken to me when you were my friend. Go away, I say, and let me alone."

And she flung off, hanging brooding on the movements of the innocent Howe and his sentimental companion. She felt the quarrel deeply. Cécile, whatever her own faults, had been Gertrude's virtue, for her she had defied her sisters and the world, and braved all things rather than shrink from avowing the unpopular connection. And now this one affection, this discredited tie to which she had been true, while she sinned against all who had served her, this was failing her, and its object joining with a humorist to laugh at her. Her heart was hot, as she drifted sulkily into the ring of guests, by this time making preparations for luncheon.

"Come now, Gertrude, be of some use, please," said Catherine hastily, not intending to speak roughly. "Hand me that jug in your hand."

Gertrude gave a little stamp with her foot and a suddenly-waked impatience made her eyes blink and her full lips tighten.

"Gertrude," repeated Catherine indignantly. "did you hear what I asked you for?"

Gertrude only stood gazing, with the jug dangling in her hand and a strange smile, but into her eyes had shot the warning spark that always threatened an outbreak.

"Gertrude," cried Catherine again, "are you deaf?" and she stretched out her hand. Gertrude fancied it was to coerce her, and at the same moment Margaret good-naturedly interposed her arm, and the youngest girl, half-blind with passion, thought that both were going to strike. She sprang back, with an inarticulate sound, and whirled up her hand. There was a flash and hurtling whirr, and the fifty fragments of the jug fell from the boss of the tree just above Catherine's head.

"Gertrude!" said Catherine and rose to her feet, staring and white with horror. The answer of the other was a mocking neigh and a leap into the briery forest. And for minutes after she disappeared they could hear her crashing through the thickets like a thing possessed.

Chapter 5

The Adventures of a Rowing-boat

"Well," Catherine Grey was saying, as the luncheon was winding up some half-hour after the last glimpse of Gertrude, "will you have any more lemonade, Mr. Fleury?"

Lucien, turning with his pale but cordial smile was about to hand in his glass with a refusal, when something fell upon it from above. It was a drop of rain.

"The gods have answered," said Margaret with the smile with which ladies quote Tennyson.

"What teetotallers those gods are," added Howe.

"Will it go on, do you think?" asked Catherine.

"No, I should think it would come back," said Howe, without in the least knowing what he meant. "To tell the truth (for a change) I am afraid it will be raining all kinds of quadrupeds directly. You had better get under shelter, I fancy, so as to have all the rain in drippings. Have you any umbrellas?"

"Yes," replied Catherine, "Margaret and I have, and Gertrude's will do for Miss Fleury. I do hope that silly girl has got into shelter at the station: she went towards it. I fancy we shall have to go home that way too. Have you got an umbrella, Mr. Howe?"

"I have no umbrella. The universe is my umbrella," replied Howe gravely. "Well, this is certainly an experience, as people say when they mean that a thing is unredeemedly nasty."

The rain as he spoke was battering down through

the dancing foliage, and tracing a gleaming wet line down the front of his tall hat, his bridged nose and stiff waistcoat, but without discomforting for a moment, with all its driving waves of water, the gaze of his cold blue eyes. "I hope you are all in shelter," he added. "Can I be of any use? The question has faced me from an early age: as the Latin Arnold says, 'Expecting the answer, No.' "

"I don't think it's any use our stopping in shelter," said Catherine, "we had much better make a dash to the station and get home."

"It is raining very hard," said her aunt suggestively.

"We are getting quite as much of it here," replied the niece. The other said no more, for her meekness mingled with a dash of fashionableness always gave way before the many-sided determination of the young house-keeper. Catherine seldom, however, remained long without seeing another side to a question, and she added suddenly, "The only thing is: what is to become of the boat?"

"Wouldn't some boat-house take it in?" asked Lucien.

"There are none within four miles," replied Catherine positively. "I am afraid we shall have to row it home again by water."

"I shouldn't row it home by land, if I were you," said Howe, doubtfully. "But as I was just going to say, when I forgot to, it is quite easy for me to row the old Témeraire to its long home, while you all go home by rail. In that case I had better see you all to the station as that is the opposite direction. Is everything ready?"

"Really, Mr. Howe," said Catherine, looking at him, "it is very kind of you to offer."

"But it will be much kinder if you let me have my

own way," he replied, hastily. "Hand me that basket, Lucien, will you. Well, this is rather moist."

They all set out in the roaring rain, a raggle-tailed, single-filing procession of umbrellas, but the whole marshalling and managing of the dismal coterie was decided in hurried conferences and monosyllables between two of the parties, the eldest girl, speeding through the lakes of rain and mud ahead of the line, and the long-legged, crowfaced young man who brought up the rear with his collar turned up. So deafening was the uproar of wind and water that they could seldom hear each other speak, and did not try, but in a part of the tired wind, through the descending columns of water, a sentence was caught by Margaret from the bland lips of Howe, "The sky looks like rain, I think."

A few moments afterwards Basil Howe was striding back alone towards the river, having left his new friends at the station. He was no pessimist for all his puckered brow, but it did cause him a reflection upon the tendencies of things, when the moment he had seen his companions disappear, the rain began to drip slower, and the sun burst out, tearing the clouds in shreds and driving them and the rain into a corner on the opposite horizon. He made no sound, however, beyond a hissing whistle between his teeth, as he swung silently along to the bank of the river along which he stepped lightly and rapidly towards the knotted and feathery willow under which the tethered boat swung up and down.

"What very nice people those are," he muttered as he caught hold of the tree and swung himself into the rocking boat. "They don't require sense from one in the least."

He began rapidly putting the ballast and light luggage to rights, bending over in the boat, and after a busy silence he said again: "Those are remarkably nice people: I never thought I should know such nice people." And then he fell to fumbling again at the equipments. While he was doing so, he heard a twig crack on the wooded slope above him and looked up. Half way up the steep above, in the shadow of the solemn ranks of pines, stood a picturesque sullen girl-figure, with frock torn with brambles, face stained with tears, and a roughened mop of red hair low over her eyes. It was Gertrude, after two hours of lonely raging amid the undergrowths of brier. Every phase of human ill-feeling had been traversed in that blind ramble, from the half-curses of selfish rage to the luxuries of sulky virtue, from the wild rehearsals of victorious taunts to the blank misery of loneliness and moral hunger. Now she came out pale and empty-hearted from her wandering wood, and saw beneath her under the bank Basil Howe, gravely and cheerfully whistling to himself as he got the boat ready for departure.

"Why, Miss Grey," he cried, when he caught sight of the solitary figure on the slope. "You are not gone home by train! Excuse the inference, but I draw it with all care and circumspection from your presence here. Can I help you down? So you have not followed your sisters?"

Gertrude was really very tired and wretched and would have been glad enough of Howe's genial nonsense, but like most people in sulk (and the condition is common enough) she felt it as a kind of dark point of honour not to give up her grievance easily, so she turned her back to him and, kicking at the bark of the tree, said, "I have not seen my sisters."

"Oh you should see your sisters," broke out Howe with enthusiasm. "They are such interesting people; besides…" Gertrude's head and back trembled and a broken billow of laughter was half-heard. Howe went on swiftly and calmly, "At any rate you had better get into the boat, unless of course you would prefer to be towed behind. Can I assist you?" and he held out his hand.

A spasm of curiosity appeared to strike Gertrude and she accepted his aid, saying, with a look at him, "Are you taking the boat home, then?"

"I'm not sure," replied he. "I rather think it is taking me. I expect we shall take it by turns, like the man and the ass; the boat representing the man, of course. I think," he said, shoving off, "that this cruise should be conducted on strictly nautical lines. I should, therefore, request you, whenever you think of it, to avast, also to pipe as many hands as Providence has seen fit to provide you with. If you have nothing else to do, it wouldn't be a bad idea to belay. I belay constantly myself. It's quite a joke against me how much I do it…."

Thus chattering everything that came into his head to cover her recovery of good spirits, they drifted for a little while before he could use the oar. There was a pause and they sat looking at each other: the one beholding a black gaunt figure in the stern, dark and watchful as a falcon against the gleaming shallows and sunset, the other looking at a slight wild figure and eager face, fiery in the warm glow of sunset as it lay half-coiled in the prow. He was surprised to notice how narrow and frail she really was. They were indeed a great contrast: a greater contrast could hardly be than that between the quick, weird, half childish girl-savage with her formless instincts and her windy vanity and her companion, the stern, tranquil, polished young man, with his sombre friendliness and his enigmatical humour: there was indeed contrast enough. But they were alike in this that they were both unfathomed, unlocked to others by the true key of their natures: and, even as they sat, they were groping at each other's.

As they drifted into the current, Gertrude said at last, "I think it is very good of you, Mr. Howe, to be taking the boat home."

"I have already pointed out," he said, tucking up his cuffs, "that it is the boat."

He took the oars and rowed on in the fading daylight: and then after a silence Gertrude spoke again, thoughtfully but abruptly, "What do you think of Mr. Fleury, Mr. Howe?" There was curiosity in her question, but it was about his character as much as Lucien's. He replied immediately, "Our cousin of Fleury is a prince of many and shining virtues. My only complaint against him is his being physically so loose: you pick up a hand of him in one place, and have to look for it again if you drop it. It is impossible to enter into concentrated and personal relations with a fellow who leaves himself about the place in that way. He is really very nice, if not considered as a whole." This was not by any means all that Howe's backbone of rationality was jarred at in Lucien and his sister, but it was all he should have ever dreamt of saying to anybody. He may not have had the sacred indignation of the prophet, he made no pretence to it. He saw through his cousins, he felt that they were weak, selfish, unstable, and liked them very well, did his best to amuse them, and would have loathed to hurt their feelings. Call it charity, call it sociability, call it paganism, it was his character.

"Do you like Cécile, Mr. Howe?" said she.

"Well you see, she is my cousin, so I hardly know her. But I notice she is a friend of yours, so I have no doubt she is the right shape. She sometimes seems flighty and — not perhaps so grovellingly humble as she might be, but she has a real feeling for what is high in her own way. So has Lucien, though he does play football. But I think Cécile is lucky in one respect."

"In what?" asked Gertrude.

"In her friends," he replied, plainly.

She felt something inside her alter its position. She had never looked upon herself as the good genius of anybody, but this dried-up stranger never paid compliments. She felt that he must really respect her, and did not dislike the idea. He rowed on, and the gloaming brooded round them, as he pushed his prow through the dark, lazy waters.

"Have you talked at all to Catherine?" she said, and her question was the third grope at his shadowy self.

"I have talked to everybody who would listen," he said grimly, "to your unhappy sister among the rest. But she made short work of me. She is a person who prefers to use speech as a hammer to using it as a baby's rattle."

She felt a faint outline of her sister in the words and her curiosity as to his criticisms was strengthened. "She is rather short at times," she said cautiously.

"Well you see, it is only yards of useless vertebrae like myself that can afford to be tall," he said thoughtfully. "She has so many journeys to make at once out of herself that she makes them all very rapid. Of course, I don't know her as well as you do, and therefore I can't admire her so much. But I feel she is a very real sort of person."

Again she felt the oddly stirring tribute of an undeserved respect, and gazed at him intently as he stared past her at the dark landscape with his bleak blue eyes. She felt her first notion that he was merely a cold, good-tempered sceptic vanishing entirely. Reverence of some kind for what was generous he had, but why was it so formal and guarded; why was his ordinary conversation simply superficial caricature? She felt the new spark in her grow fiercer, curiosity to solve this riddle, Basil Howe. She looked again at the dark face of her sphinx, and ventured on a personal question. "Are you stopping here for the season, Mr. Howe?" she asked.

"As far as I know I am here not for an age but all time," he said. "My faithful and attached father, who is now in America, has directed me to make arrangements with my poor cousins that I should stop with them (compensation for the injury being of course secured them) until I have learnt Law and made all the necessary professional arrangements for justifying the wicked for reward and taking away the righteousness of the righteous from him. On my appearance at the Bar and consequent selection for the post of Lord Chief Justice, I shall probably go to see my father, leaving my cousins in tears. I have hitherto shared with them a cottage in Gloucester Place, and on their coming down to this rugged ocean shore, I am still found faithful and share my crust with my dear kind master. I am in short a boarder, somewhat in the same aggressive sense as the word is applied to the capturer of a pirate vessel. That is my life, Miss Grey."

Gertrude spoke before she reflected, "Do you like it?" she said eagerly.

"Oh, I am about as happy as a King or a sandboy, or a sunbeam or any other of those happy things is, I should think. In other words, Kismet."

She did not quite understand, nor did he, but her brow seemed troubled and he hastened to clear it.

"I am really more sane than you would suppose," he said, with a smile. "You need not apologise: many people have thought that my upper story was not such a perfect specimen of the tiler's art as it might be. But I shan't do you any harm, I assure you." The last words were of the random character of his lighter speech, but there was a ring of half-meaning in them. The mystery of the man seemed to thicken as his kindness looked out at odd cracks. She wanted to ask him another question, but had a fear of him, lest persistent questioning should offend him. Then, as was characteristic of her feeling towards him, she felt instantly impelled to put the question, to see if he would be offended.

"Mr. Howe," she asked, "do you want to be a barrister?"

"Well, you see," he said confidentially, "I have received such pressing invitations from the Lord Chancellor, and Mr. Gladstone too, you see, put it so much as a personal favour to him, that I really had no peace till I consented. The importunity of those kind of people, Miss Grey, is extraordinary."

Gertrude looked at him with a sort of dreamy pleasure. Whatever he was, he was illimitably good-tempered. He had answered without even seeing that her question was almost impertinent.

"And here we are at the boat-house," said he, as

they swung to and fro on the swell within reach of the pillars of the house. "Will you just hand me that post," he said to her; she grasped it and drove the boat under it till it was in his hands, and the prow of the boat against the shore. And as he helped her out, with a queer sentence that made her laugh again, she knew that she had made a friend, though a friend she could not yet fully understand.

Chapter 6

The Day of Rest

The next day being Sunday Mr. Basil Howe arose at his usual early hour and dressed with his usual care and neatness in his usual, decent, aged clothes. No human being was ever less of a dandy in the conscious sense, but his invariable accuracy of exterior was part of a certain intellectual thoroughness which appeared in everything he did. His habits were unobtrusive, regular, like his costume.

Having assumed the shabby but well-brushed hat (which he never changed) and unearthed a shabby but well-kept prayer-book, he betook himself with his usual silent swiftness to church, not so much it is to be feared from a consciously religious motive as from a taciturn love of the society of his fellow creatures which was his most salient characteristic.

"I am in time for the overture," he muttered as he took his seat in a side pew. "Hullo! Mark of the beast," he observed promptly, catching sight of a great cross over the altar. "Sadly high, sadly high. Well, here's for the Gregorian jokes and all the attendant incantations for summoning the Eternal Spirit of the Universe." Howe was not satirising, he never did so: it was always the abstract humour of conception that attracted him, absolutely never the desire to attack anything.

Turning his head, he glanced round the small but crowded church, and his sharp eyes rested for a moment, with a sudden gleam, on three bright maiden heads, aureoled in the sunlight, the heads of the Greys in their family pew. What his thoughts were as his stern blue eyes rested so long on the three unconscious haloed ones, we cannot fully analyse, but they were stirred very deep, and mingled of that hushed sensation of sacredness, purity, completeness, which an honest *family*, even more than an individual, conveys to those who can feel it. Let no one blame Howe for such thoughts in church; the interest in our churchgoing neighbours, so far from being the decadent, is almost the only genuine Christian thing left in modern conventional piety: a real echo of the early believers, whose meals and meetings of fellowship were entirely free of the sacramental awe which afterwards crept in from Paganism.

"The Countess of Greencroft looks as if her religion doesn't agree with her," he said, scrutinising anxiously the palely-tinted earnest profile and black hair of Catherine. "I do hope we didn't knock her up, to use a technical phrase, yesterday. Lady Margaret appears to have adopted a more cheerful theology. As to my honourable friend beyond, doctrine is hardly in her line. I have heard that she is what ethnologists would term a tartar. She has been quite polite to me, which argues some capabilities of character, but I think it can't be altogether a libel. Yes, I think she certainly belongs to the Mongolian branch."

"From pride and vain-glory, from hardness of heart, from envy, malice, and all uncharitableness, Good Lord deliver us," said the litany, and Howe, generally wide-awake and the reverse of abstracted, found they were in the middle of it, and joined in. He did not think much of the service, however: three glory-crowned figures were his religion at the moment (a more genuine one than some) and one, wilder, more magnetic, more troublesome than the other two, over whom her new friend's thoughts lingered with the forethought and the interest of an elder brother.

The three girls had knelt too, but it may be doubted whether they prayed much more than he, even without his excuse for abstraction. This may seem a harsh thing to say, but it is my duty to suggest carefully a very typical and noble set of English girls, and the truth must be told. I do not think they had anything that could be called personal religion. Howe had much more of it in his inward, rational way. Cécile herself had more of it, a morbid ecstatic kind of religion, when she went to her Roman Catholic chapel. Personal religion seems in this way often the possession of the orphan, the nomad, the man of the world, but hundreds of children like these are brought up in sane, well-ordered families, without ever thinking of religion as anything but a vague, beautiful, correct thing, to be recognised as a matter of course.

The Epistle was almost the only thing in the service itself that Howe heeded or remembered. It was St. Paul's exaltation of Love and some of the sentences rang through his head. For the sermon he always waited with the interest of a keenly intellectual nature, given up to the study of books and theories, and bad or good it always gave him something to think about. That Sunday it was not exactly either: a noisy rather clever man was asking for money, banging the pulpit to make the money jump out of the pockets of the congregation, vociferating at the roof for not contributing to the collection. He pronounced the name of Christ rather as a highway man might hurl the watchword of his gang, as a menace to the traveller, he was evidently honestly, turbulently convinced that his particular church debt had an inexhaustible right to all the private property assembled in the church: he appeared perpetually jumping on the dead body of an objection.

Howe's clear eyes never blinked during these mendicant thunders, but remained decently, respectfully, coldly fixed on the purple face of the holy man, but when the congregation thronged out and the Greys met him in the porch and asked him what he thought of it he replied readily.

"O, an unctious minister, I think," he said, reminiscent of his youth in Scotland. "Very savoury doctrine too, really very savoury doctrine."

"Mr. Howe," said Gertrude quietly, "what do you really think of the sermon?"

He instantaneously forgot the other two and spoke to a nature he partially understood. "Oh, he was a trifle perturbed, I allow," he said. "But there was a manliness about him and his shamelessness, for all that. He was better than the whining curate, for he did mean something if it was only money. I don't care much for that sort of sermon though. If a man asked for money in that way for his father or brother in daily life, he would be set in life as a cad at once. Why should a man forget courtesy and decency because he is not going to pocket the money himself? Why need a man do good in that swaggering way? If I give all my substance in alms and have not love it availeth me nothing, as Julius Caesar, I think, remarked."

A scriptural quotation, even with that extraordinary tail to it, seemed new from those dry, light-speaking lips, and she glanced quickly at his mask of bronze which told her less than ever.

"I never liked him myself," she said, with a curious feeling of encouragement.

"I suppose he wants the money," said Catherine with a kind of sympathy with the practical worker.

"I should say there can be no doubt," said Howe, passively, "that he wants that. In fact, to tell the truth, he as good as hinted at it in the sermon."

Margaret laughed, "He is a curious sort of man, I know. He won't take off his hat, for instance, to ladies he knows, because he is a clergyman."

A sharp look of disgust, not often seen there shot across Howe's visage, but he spoke almost indifferently, "I don't see the sense of that altogether. My natural faculties for knowing sense when I see it are not large, but that seems to me an unnecessary piece of dignity, like most pieces. He wouldn't be the first gentleman connected with Christianity who took notice of women (you haven't got any wells in this soil, have you?) and he won't be the last. I don't object to any man having a high opinion of his office. I shall have the very highest opinion of my office when I find out what it is, but I think if he were the Pope of Rome he might take off – his tiara."

The conversation then swimming for a little between Howe and Catherine was almost entirely light and laughing. Margaret and Gertrude looked on with a certain surprise; they always stood to some extent in awe of their able, serious, high-minded eldest sister, they had never met anyone who could tackle her, and they felt a kind of excitement in watching the way in which this daring, humorous man of the world took her severity by the horns, and with perfect tact and courtesy, carried her off laughing at his breezy converse, in a way which neither they nor their acquaintances would have dared to attempt. Only once he went beyond her, when in answer to a question about Emerson's poetry he said, "Yes, I have tried it. I am bound, however, to say that I found it somewhat in the condition of the bones of Ezekiel. It was very dry."

Catherine looked grave for she had been brought up to a disapproval of irreverence, of which the conversational wanderer had never felt the weight: but her silence was interrupted by a loud ringing laugh, approving, defiant, protective. It was from Gertrude. Gertrude was, however, mistaken if she thought Catherine was offended, for she was not: first because she was by this time really fond of her dark, talkative companion, secondly because she, being a well brought-up girl, was not in a position in which people commonly analyse their friends or consider them as characters to be studied. This stage of the conversation brought them to the door where the Greys were met by their aunt, Miss Thornton.

"Well," said that lady, undulating with that peculiar motion which expresses the pleasure of certain mildly fashionable people. "And did Mr. Jacks give you a good sermon?"

"Oh so nice," said Howe cordially. "He stood quite up on his hind legs in the pulpit and begged."

That afternoon Lucien, Cécile, Gertrude and Howe went for a country scramble together over the immense downs and billows of land that lay along the edge of the cliffs above the sea, Howe earnestly characterising every giant change of the bare landscape as a thing which it might be doubted whether you could see in

Paddington from one year's end to another. It was an absurd flourish of the commonplace comment to which he was occasionally addicted.

That evening Gertrude was to go to tea with Cécile, so that on their return, she sat for the first but not by any means the last time at the same tea-table as her new friend. Afterwards during their stay next door to each other it came to be regarded as a usage that the two families had tea to some extent at each other's houses. It was a happy time for all of them, when Cécile and Gertrude would come bounding down the staircase to tea, when Margaret threw down her book to join them, when Catherine rapid and radiant was pouring out the tea, and Howe flitting behind everybody with interminable bread and butter and comments and explanations that made them all nearly choke over it. It was a very happy and a very honest time in all their lives, and only two of them had a restless thought. One of these was Gertrude and her restless thought was that for all his serviceableness and good humour there was a reserve force in Howe, a locked chamber: a closed door behind which was stored what would explain him: and the thought to this wilful girl was a spur. The other was Howe: but what his restless thought was Gertrude might not then know, nor may we.

One evening when Howe came home from a walk he found a letter awaiting him, addressed in a round good hand, with too strong a feeling of the schoolroom in it. He slit it open and found a card on which was written: "Miss Grey requests the pleasure of Mr. Basil Howe's company to an evening party on Tuesday the 17th instant. Dancing. R.S.V.P." He looked at this note for a moment, and then put it carefully onto his bedroom mantelpiece. Coming back again to it, he stared at it again with inexplicable knitted brows, and all through his subsequent engagement of putting his books to rights came continually back, duster in hand, to stare at the card on his mantelpiece. The restless thought was on him.

Chapter 7

The Confession of Basil Howe

On Tuesday the 17th instant, as the card expressed it, late in the afternoon, Gertrude sat kicking her heels on the sofa, having in her lap a furry white kitten. And this kitten had a history. One day during the previous week Howe had offered to show her his books, and, with a flutter of excitement as to the private equipments of her unsearchable walking riddle, she went up the staircase. His room was dark, neat and quiet, like the dress and manner of its occupant, a couple of book-shelves, home-made but sound, held two ranks of well used volumes: a set of Browning, two or three novels of Thackeray, Stevenson's "New Arabian Nights" and a pocket volume of Walt Whitman: these were the most prominent. A small dark print from Albert Dürer hung on the wall, while a couple of fencing foils in the corner were the only tribute to athleticism. A square stout trunk stood under the window, capable under the powerful and experienced packing of its owner of holding all these "effects" as he was in the habit of calling them. Everything suggesting a solitary, self-reliant existence. All these, however, she noticed less at first than another object which sprawled and rolled to the middle of the rug. The moment she saw it, with the impulsive naturalness that guided her always, she gave a cry of pleasure and sprang onto her knees, the white kitten kicking in her arms.

"Ah, you've got Robert Ellesmere," said Howe casually. "Shall I show you the other kittens? Hi! hi!"

Two more kittens, one black and the other white scampered from behind the trunk, and Gertrude, happily unconscious of her picturesque situation, was sitting in the middle of the rug laughing with the three romping quadrupeds. "What did you call that one?" she asked, looking up with dancing eyes.

"That kitten with the sincere and abstracted air is Robert Ellesmere. I think more thought and seriousness should be expended on the naming of kittens, and mine are all carefully drawn from contemporary literature. That more frisky and excited character goes by the name of Evan Harrington. As for this lady," indicating the black kitten, "I have designated her 'Hedder Gabla'. Her moral state is not good. She scratched me the other day, and did it beautifully. You seem very much taken up with Robert Ellesmere. He has one advantage over his prototype. If he has doubts he keeps them to himself. He is a good kitten."

"He is a lovely one," said Gertrude, brushing its hair for it. "Where did you get him?"

"I really forget," he replied. "But I expect I stole him. I don't know whether you would care to have the kitten, Miss Grey, but if you like you can steal him yourself. I shan't be looking."

"Oh may I really have him, Mr. Howe," cried Gertrude, springing erect and excited with the kitten in her arms.

"Oh yes," he replied, "you can go and make an orthodox churchman of him if you like, and drag him to church with a white ribbon."

Before he had finished his sentence, she had gushed out a word of gratitude and gone dashing downstairs with the kitten. Some people would have been offended at her abruptness and neglect of his presence, but Howe was glad enough to please anyhow, and only gave an odd little laugh as he went on dusting his books.

This was the history of the white kitten that lay in Gertrude's lap as she sat on the sofa in slim, white, square-necked evening attire, with a red ribbon. She was much too early for the arrivals, but her excited anticipations had hurried her. She looked forward to the party as she had looked forward to no other; had she analysed her own feelings (which she never did, though occasionally other people's) she would have felt a pride in a new and striking friend to show off: a brilliant tongue, a powerful and original mind of her own discovering, to enjoy the effect of on other people. The best proof that her attraction to Basil Howe was purest honest friendship lay in the fact that she had never hitherto wished to have him to herself: her greatest pleasure in life was to watch other people amused and pleased with him.

Being of this habit, it must remain a mystery why she was distressed, all but ill-tempered, during the earlier part of the evening. He was there, dancing, with portentous gravity, first with Catherine, then with Cécile, then with Margaret, then with strangers, then with her, then with Catherine again. His evening dress was as straight and square a piece of black and white as his ordinary clothes, his steely eyes and falcon face were as changeless as ever, his talk as quaint and startling as of old. Yet Gertrude felt burning, nervous, on end; she did not feel that all was going as she had hoped: she felt a hitherto unknown bitterness creeping into her, as he darted round the crowded room; and as the evening wore on, and through all her fretting hours, she was shadowed by Lucien Fleury, like a pale and inviting Mephistopheles in his full shirt front and yellow rose, smart but artistic, and his egoistic but not thoughtless chatter maddening her ears. He was always speaking personally and sentimentally; give him half an hour with any civil companion and he was in the abysses of confidences. I do not sneer at him for this, I think his honesty and companionable simplicity very much the best thing about him. But to Gertrude it was barren as wind, and she grew more and more evil-tempered. Why she was so disappointed with the scene must remain a mystery, one of those untouched places of a woman's heart, but it was something that stung her whenever she saw Howe's proud yellow face moving among the crowds, and the sting was a question put to herself.

"Of course one must dance," Lucien was saying easily, "but upon my word it's a great bore. I don't care for it myself, do you?"

"No," said Gertrude fiercely, as Howe span down the room with Cécile in fits of laughter. The next moment the two had parted and Howe was standing before her. "Can I have the pleasure of treading on your toes again, Miss Grey?" he said politely.

Gertrude, by this time quite sore for no reason whatever, remembered her words to Lucien and replied sulkily, "No thank you Mr. Howe. I don't care for any more dancing."

"You look rather tired," he replied submissively. "Shall we go into the conservatory?" and he passed on to open the glass door for her. Gertrude followed him, getting more and more angry. The root of her discontent was her baffled attempt to fathom him, mixed with a kind of suspicion, and under these feelings his bleak face and placid manner enraged her. They found themselves alone in the close green conservatory and Howe spoke, "I think you had better have the window open, it is like a green hole of Calcutta."

Her spirit being in its evil cloud, she only felt, "He thinks he can beat me and make me laugh: can he!"

"That's a new expression," she said, chilly.

"Is it?" he replied. "If so, I should have been glad of it five minutes ago."

"What were you doing then?" asked Gertrude sharply.

"I was having the exquisite honour of dancing with your friend Cécile," he said with a humorous look. "At least, I thought so. It must have been somebody else."

Gertrude, finding herself again beating against a closed door, that barred door of his being which was sentinelled by a jester, flew wild again and cried out, "What do you know about Cécile: and what has she got to do with you?" The next moment she felt that her speech had been rude, reckless, disgraceful, and that she had given the argument into his hands. She waited sullenly for the answer.

After a pause he spoke quite humbly: "I have noticed an interesting usage in your family: that of being right. I had no business to speak against your friend. I hope you will forgive me."

She saw the aim of his words as he swept them past her, and her pride broke in her heart she saw that, where nine good people out of ten would have crushed her with a melodramatic piece of wounded nobleness, he had quickly formulated his reply so as to put himself in the wrong, smooth down her ruffled feathers and efface her humiliation from her thoughts. It may not have been correct in principle: it may not have been "for her good", but the self-denial of it was undeniable: and it went through her like a keen wind. She bit her lip, dropt her face into shadow and walked fidgeting to the other end of the conservatory and back again. When she stood in front of him her cheeks were wet and she spoke with a little difficulty. He had not gone, that would have been a touch of the injured heroism he avoided, but sat mildly playing with a piece of bamboo, with his eyes fixed on the ground.

"Mr. Howe," said Gertrude in a very little voice.

"Miss Grey," he said, hastily looking up.

"Mr. Howe," she said brokenly, "I hope you will forgive me. I was very silly and unfair, and you were altogether right and never said so. I hope you know, for all my bad tempers, that I should be as sorry as any of us, to lose as good a friend to us all as you are."

His face was bent towards the ground during this appeal, darkened and knotted in a kind of thought.

"Mr. Howe," said Gertrude, "do you understand?"

"Yes, Miss Grey," he said, but his face was still drawn and dark.

"Very well then," said Gertrude with a trembling little laugh, like one who throws off an ugly dream. "Let us come into the drawing-room. People will be wanting us there."

He laughed shortly and it sounded strange to her, being the first time she had heard it, and unlike his other tones the laugh was bitter.

"I have no doubt, Miss Grey," he said, "that they will be wanting you: but as for me, I fancy that generation will go down to its laudors in peace, without seeing me."

He spoke in his usual hard voice, but something like a break in it made her look at him quickly, and she saw an expression on his features that she had never seen there before.

"What is the matter?" she cried.

"Nothing," he said in a strong, grinding voice, and his dark face was working with passion.

"There is something," persisted Gertrude gently. "You are our friend and we are pleased to help you. What is the matter? What have I said?"

He began again, by profound effort, in his decided tones, and then his voice failed him altogether. Then a low, hoarse, random voice, seeming to come from a deeper and different part of his body, shaped the half-articulate expression, "… Oh… it's nothing… I was only wondering what it would feel like to have known a human being who cared whether I lived or died."

Gertrude trembled from head to foot with the shock of a revelation. She could hardly tell what it was she had seen, but she had a knowledge, a sensation rather than a thought, but a sensation not vague but acute, that she had come upon something immeasurably splendid and sorrowful: that the barred door had given way before her and given her a glimpse into a vast silence.

Before she could speak, Howe, after what can only be described as a sharp wrestle with his own voice and lips, regained his composure and said with a certain dignity, "I beg your pardon, Miss Grey, for my drivelling talk. I had forgotten myself for a moment and relieved my mental bag indiscreetly of its feline occupant. Shall we go into the drawing-room, then?"

Gertrude answered in a vague and shaking voice. "No… no," she said half wildly. "Tell me what is the matter, Mr. Howe. Why do you say that?"

"I am only reverentially repeating the already

efficient work of the Creator by making a fool of myself," he replied, and set his teeth hard.

"Mr. Howe," replied Gertrude, with no little shrewdness. "You seem to have corked yourself up too much, and it will do you good to have it out. Will you do me a favour by conquering your disgust and telling me more? It is not often I ask for anything."

Nothing in the seven heavens save that one small last sentence would have made Howe add another word to an involuntary outbreak for which he loathed himself: but he had an instinct, an engrained habit rather, of putting himself second to the person he was talking to, and he thought of her.

He began with an heroic effort at his ordinary manner, "Once upon a time..." and then a rush of thoughts seemed to break up his iron voice once more, and again the low faltering speech crept out, "... Well, you know what sort of person I am, Miss Grey... I know I seem stuck-up and talk nonsense, and everybody, of course, dislikes me. The worst of it is that they are right in disliking me. I don't mean to be stuck-up, but I do talk blatant folly: I daren't talk anything else, when I know everyone despises me. I used to think it didn't so much matter, so long as I could mix with good people, and perhaps – perhaps make them laugh a little with my idiocy: and I used, being a fool, you know, to be a little proud of not minding being a cipher – of cutting my silly antics patiently when I felt ever so low. It was – a wretched vanity; but I – I am telling you everything, and a fellow clings to a rag of pride when he has no one to care for him. Of course, no one ever cared for me: it is my fault totally for acting like an owl: but my bed was made and I lay on it... but then... then I met some people who were cleverer and franker and more generous than anyone I had ever known: and I forgot my own folly in watching them… and I let myself admire them and feel one of them more and more…, and then," he spoke low, but there was a cry in his voice, "… then I remembered. I remembered I was a wretched cheap society pantaloon, and that they would think as everyone else had thought. If I could have come the neglected merit joke, it would have been less bitter: but I couldn't. They were so much better than I in every way: they had a right to laugh: they did nothing they had not a right to do…." His voice seemed to lose itself in darkness, and the last words were as if to himself. "… I am telling this now to one of them… and she must be laughing." There was a stillness and he broke the bamboo sharply between his hands.

Gertrude stood hot under her chestnut hair and breathing hard as the long-sealed nature poured itself brokenly before her from the core of a great loneliness. When she spoke it was carefully, softly, with something shining in her eyes. "Mr. Howe," she said very cautiously, "why do you think nobody cares for you?"

He made a kind of sound between a laugh and a groan. "Do you feel a yearning to be introduced to the clown at the pantomime?" he asked. "Have I ever said or suggested anything that anybody should like? Have I ever said a serious word of love or hate to any mortal creature? Have I ever given anyone any reason to suppose that I had any ideas upon any subject or any feelings towards any person? People came to me and talked till they were nauseated and then went away. What is there for anyone to like? It may be doubted," he added suddenly, as if recovering a scornful power over himself, "whether I was the sorriest fool then or now: I think now on the whole. But the load was growing very bitter. You had only to touch it with the end of your finger… I have never spoken of it in my life before: till you spoke so good-naturedly just now… I never will speak of it again…." And he drummed on the table.

Gertrude stood in shadow above him and her hair was like a glory, red passionate with fire, and in her eyes was a dazzling misty light. As she rose, looking down on the lonely and broken figure, the child had become a woman.

"Mr. Howe," she said softly and firmly, "would you believe me if I said something quite sincerely?"

"I know you always speak the truth," he replied without lifting his head.

"Then listen to me," she said earnestly: forgetting conventions, as she had forgotten self. "It's not true, what you think. We do like you very truly and very much. I think you are very noble and thoughtful of other people: as well as clever and amusing. I never met anyone who gave up himself all so much as you. Catherine will give up her wishes often, but she never gives up herself: her ways of looking at it, as you do. I do think it indeed," she cried passionately, in almost maternal compassion, "and so do Catherine and Margaret and Cécile, I know they do. And even if they didn't –" she paused and a mist came across her eyes.

He had not raised his darkened countenance during this answer, but he was quick to feel realities, and the obscurity of bitterness was gone from his attitude and it was the obscurity of a new birth of emotions that crept up in dark red in his sun-browned cheek and brow.

"You say it is true," he said in a trembling voice, "and you always speak the truth. If it is true... I can only say you have made me very happy, happier than I ever was in my life. I could not have believed it before.... I can hardly believe it now.... Miss Grey, can you really stand me – and be my friend?"

"Yes, Mr. Howe," she said very sweetly and fearlessly, giving him her hand. "I have told you it is true: it is quite true."

Howe took her hand and wrung it sharply. "Miss Grey," he began in his own genuine humility, but at this point Margaret entered the conservatory, smiling with frank curiosity.

"What are you up to here, Mr. Howe?" she asked. Howe sprang politely to his feet and there was a change in his features as the putting on of a mask.

"Oh, pray excuse us," he said with a gesture towards the conservatory window and the pitch darkness outside, "we were admiring the view."

This is the story of how Basil Howe, at the age of nineteen, made his first friend.

Chapter 8

Love Is the Fulfilling of the Law

A few moments afterwards Gertrude was back in the ball room seated between Margaret and Lucien, and Howe had shot off to claim a dance with Catherine. Her two neighbours were chattering away to her, but she did not feel angered with them as before, though her eyes and thoughts were following Howe round the room. Had she remembered her dark temper of half-an-hour ago she would have been ashamed of it, but she had forgotten everything in a heart that was beating with a new world of interest and knowledge. As she watched Howe going from group to group and leaving them in laughter, making the party by his own unnoticed efforts, she felt a kind of swelling pride in him: pride such as she had of old in his humour: but now a thousand times keener. Her cheek flushed and her eyes swam most of all as she noticed, out of her new knowledge of him, that he never gave her a glance, that he never let a gleam of his late passion show through his formality: the brave lonely society jester had pulled on his motley hood over his face again and was going patiently through his work. The dance went on and it at last began to break up, but in every stage and group of its dissolution Gertrude felt the broad throbs of a new happiness in life. Her heart went out kindly to the breathless, laughing, weak-kneed Lucien, as he limped up to say good night: after a dizzy evening of "going it"; she felt a kind of pure sisterly compassion as she kissed Cécile departing: a pity for her friend who could not know her happiness till she also was in the secret of a friend. Two more girls and a dark gentle-looking lad came up to take farewell: Gertrude had never seen them before, but she took their hands with something like affection, as if everyone were good if you knew them. Then Howe slid up and offered his hand to Catherine, with a grave phrase that made her eyes laugh: then she heard him say, shaking hands with Margaret, "You will hardly like Sir Roger de Coverly so much after that last dance of ours." She said something bright in answer and Howe took a step to Gertrude. As he took her hand he seemed inclined to pass on with some trifling remark: paused a moment, and said, staring half-embarrassed at the ground with a faint smile, "You shall try the experiment if you like, Miss Grey." She pressed his hand hard and he whipt away and went flying at a run through the dark streets.

And for fourteen days and nights after that Gertrude reigned in the kingdom of her secret, sat dreaming by herself of the silent and loyal friend who had brought a new meaning into her life. Her sisters were surprised to find her so quiet, the more so because she generally was exceptionally fractious and violent after a great outing or festivity. She went about, perfectly gentle and obliging, she was rather busy and appeared perfectly happy. Her office of friend and confident of the lonely and heart-hungry "man of mirth" was by no means altogether a cheerful one. With ceaseless cursings of himself for troubling her, Howe could not help letting her see when the recurring shadow of his own unworthyness vexed him, and whenever she saw it, she ransacked heaven and earth and employed every wile and phrase of her woman's tongue to brighten his thoughts of his position and persuade him of his own popularity. He drifted unconsciously towards her whenever his heart was heavy, and she hardly needed to be told, with such utter knowledge did she now read those dauntless eyes which had baffled her before. The whirling paradoxes, the odd stories of side knowledge, the cranks of expression and squibs of information were now almost entirely given to others: to Catherine and the rest: for Gertrude were the half-uttered sentences, the long-hoarded husky emotions, the spasmodic doubts and hopes of a novice in friendship: these were her melancholy portion, and she was more proud of it than of any conceivable compliment. Sometimes he half groaningly expressed to her a dread that he was depressing her with his self-dislike: sometimes the same thing crossed her own mind: and her comment was a proud defiant thought rising in her heart, which said half-articulately, "... and if it should make me ever so wretched ... rather so...." To understand her exultation in their private relation, it must be remembered that Gertrude's character was quite raw: that she was a child, a savage, with nothing but her feelings to guide her: that in her case the good bringing-up had left sleeping the large capacities of her nature and that now they were coming blundering forth. Compassion and admiration swayed them, and no human being will ever know the education that they were: the masterly attainment of tact, invention and good temper which Gertrude found easy when her heart led her in those days: the total disappearance, to the puzzling of her friends, of the "mad" Gertrude who had only been the idle Gertrude. Whatever their relationship may have been as a whole, there can be no doubt that during that period the inexperienced girl was the stronger and the comforter. Howe, the whimsical social conversationalist, knew this well and if ever a quiet young man of the 19th century was a grovelling idolator in private, Mr. Basil Howe was such at this period. Rent and unstrung, as many men are for a little, by the very shock of a new sympathy and by the momentary loosening of his life-long grip upon himself, he had for a few days afterwards practically one thought: adoration of her who had thrown a word to him. Gertrude's feeling, on the other hand, went beyond the present into schemes and theories for recasting her existence, crude and childish for the most part. In all sorts of ways, her raw energy showed itself. The Grey family, like most middle-class families of the same type, was Conservative in politics, Conservative of the high-minded domestic kind; Howe, however, it was discovered, was a Liberal: and shortly afterwards Gertrude emerged as a Red Republican of the most flaring and unreasonable type, and shook the domestic tea-table with youthful and somewhat narrow denunciations of the Royal Family, and spoke of the nationalisation of land as of something she could assist at the next morning. At another time she was found taking up an extreme position with regard to the existence of humour in heaven, which Catherine disapproved of, and Margaret laughed at. But rude as may have been her attempts to begin her new life, there was a personal quality in them that did not exist in the traditional honour of her sisters. There was not among the old children of obedience a nobler type than theirs, but she that was least in the Kingdom of Heaven is greater than they.

Chapter 9

In Which a Bird Takes Wing

A party of five young people were plodding in file along the straggling, heath-fringed edge of the cliffs above a depth of sleepy blue. Margaret, laden as in some tireless way she always contrived to be, with books from the library, walked ahead with Cécile: behind the light felt hat and lightest of his seven light suits, the decorations of Lucien, contrasted with the eternal square black hat and long black coat of his cousin Howe. And between the two groups Gertrude hovered like a happy moth, propounding laughing fads and nostrums to everyone.

Howe, as we have said, was far from a silent person; his habit, as he himself described it, was rather that of the cuttle-fish: "who conceals his general ugliness and fatuity of behaviour from the eyes of more dignified radiates by emitting obscurities": but though he still kept Lucien in the convulsions of an antic skeleton, there were times on this walk when he seemed to ask nothing better than to gaze silently at Gertrude, as the wind billowed and rolled her flame-coloured hair, decoratively relieved against the dreamy blue of the sea.

"I observe you are ready for your landlord," said Howe to Lucien (who had been shunted off onto his uncomplaining cousin, when everyone else dreaded a confidential tirade). "I compliment you. Business habits should be kept up," and he indicated the gun which Lucien carried slung over his arm.

It is a curious fact that everyone who carries a gun or a fishing-rod, has a look of reflected importance, as if there was some heroism in the position: and Lucien looked trebly so because of his intense worship of the "manly" sports of his age. But for the dash of French noblesse in him, which gave him his aesthetic sense, he was a very common type of young Englishman, lean, pale, athletic, like a person eternally on a pedestrian tour. Perhaps he was more like the older schoolboy at the rather selfish age than anything else; like him he was utterly weak in the matter of fashion, flirtation, and even mild whispers of vice, but like him he was chivalrous in a way, possessed of plenty of good feeling, and utterly incapable of keeping his secrets to himself. We say this word as to his character, because he was just then on the eve of a sight, which suggested to him an action which brought much in its train. The sight was when, attracted by a cry of pleasure from Gertrude, he turned and saw a gold-finch dart from the undergrowth: the action was to catch his gun smartly and cock.

"What are you doing?" screamed Gertrude. "You are not going to hurt it?" Lucien stared and laughed. He was not cruel, except with the cruelty of the schoolboy and the Englishman, the cruelty of thoughtless usage; but he could not comprehend the tenderness of an animal lover like Gertrude. He made to step backwards towards the place.

"Mr. Fleury!" gasped Gertrude and caught tight hold of his wrist. His answer was another resolute laugh, for the frenzy of sport was upon him, and moreover, he never contemplated really being influenced by a girl's mind. He disengaged himself courteously and darted back, gun in hand. Gertrude swayed to and fro like a reed, in a sick helplessness, and called on her sisters inarticulately, "... Margaret... Cécile... for God's sake stop it."

"Stop what?" asked Cécile wonderingly.

"Your brother – the bird," choked Gertrude, screwing her eyes like one in terror of a sight.

A sharp dark spasm, more of pain than of anger altered Howe's features for a moment, and pulling his hat-brim over his eyes he sped silently after Lucien and said something to him. They were out of ear-shot, but the three girls watching the two lean dark figures confronting one another against the sky, could almost fancy the mental conflict, and feel the fiery, hunting, fighting aristocratically inherited instincts of the son of mediaeval counts cowed before the keen promptitude and experienced capacity of the representative of an educated middle class. Howe seemed to be saying something with unusual slowness and severity, to which Lucien replied with an evil laugh over his shoulder. Then the other bowed and Lucien threw the gun over his shoulder and they returned. Gertrude was standing flushed up to the roots of her hair, with bright teeth and shining peacock eyes, in a kind of trance of emotion. Her hero-worship had just risen to the highest point of all.

As they turned at this point and walked homeward Howe's conversation to Gertrude and the others was more varied and fanciful than ever. He seemed perfectly prodigal of his gargantuan sentences and suggestions. Only insignificant scraps remained in Gertrude's throbbing brain and can be transcribed here. Somehow or other they were in the middle of a discussion about animals and Margaret was drawing attention to a host of ants (for she was fond of natural history) overcrowded and kicking in the hole. "Dear me: what Malthusians there must be there," he said in a distressed voice, "and here comes some more: 'Go to the ant' as his late majesty King Solomon remarked, being I suppose the Aramaic equivalent for 'go to the deuce'. 'Go to Jericho' is doubtless another monument of Semitic delicacy."

"Go to the Ants: it should have said," remarked Margaret. "You'll hardly find one to yourself."

"So it would no doubt have been said, had I been consulted all along. But to tell you the truth, the fact is I never wrote the Book of Proverbs myself, the rumour is entirely an unfounded one which attributes the authorship to me. Had it simply said that I had revised and corrected it, I should have been quite content."

"You are content now, aren't you," said Gertrude with a look between jest and earnest.

"Oh yes," he said cheerfully, but after a wince, "I have really only one thing to wish for: and there not being any piebald horses loose about the landscape or any new moons and glass windows provided, I will leave it unuttered. And now, Miss Grey," he said, pausing to their general astonishment at a stile that led to the station, "To coin a phrase, Goodbye."

"Where are you going?" cried Margaret, staring. "Why make a halt at this stile?"

"Because I want to get to the other side, as the web-footed humorist said to the enquiring traveller. As to where I am going, I hardly know. Mayhap to that Great Stile – but no matter. In other words, I am going to London."

"To London ... you!" repeated Margaret and Cécile in a breath. Gertrude was standing behind them, every dash of colour had dropt out of her eager face, and her elvish features seemed carven in white ivory under her fierce red tresses. Howe held out his hand to her. Her strange green eyes leapt at something and held it. "Mr. Howe," she said, breathlessly in a low tone, "what did you say to Mr. Fleury?"

"He will tell you," replied Howe, blinking at the home thrust. Lucien was not chary of information and she afterwards learnt that Howe, knowing persuasion useless, had threatened to strike: quarrelled in fact and repeated it, as it were with his trunk packed.

Afterwards Gertrude treasured passionately the recollection of the extreme menace and renunciation that her hero had made for her wish, but now she was hardly conscious of it. The whole world had become suddenly black.

"Goodbye, Miss Grey," said Howe to Margaret, with one foot on the stile. "Goodbye, Cécile: my holiday is up."

"I am very sorry it is," said Margaret, sincerely, almost earnestly, for her sense and humour had always been drawn towards this "character" as she called him. Howe looked at her with troubled eyes that cleared at last. "I really believe you are just now," he said slowly. "However, we'll soon alter all that. Goodbye." He shook hands slowly, almost tenderly with Margaret and Cécile, caught Gertrude's cold hand with a sharp compression, cleared the stile with his old dazzling agility, and set off walking hard towards the station.

"It's a very sudden exit," said Margaret. "I suppose he'll call for his trunk on his way. Well, where shall we go now? Where's Gertrude?" She was only dawdling in front, kicking the sand up with her feet.

"We had better get home, Gertrude," called out

Margaret; "Miss Amiens, you know, might come to tea. You remember them at the party, the mild dark young gentleman and his sisters."

"Mr. Amiens is a fool," said Gertrude in a loud voice.

Lucien began to laugh in a startled, silly sort of way, and Margaret wrinkled her clear forehead. The visitors did not come to tea, and Catherine coming in late for that meal from a round of calls partook of it alone with Gertrude who was sprawling restlessly on the sofa.

"But why aren't you going with us all up the river?" Catherine was asking. "It will be certain to be fine weather."

"It'll be sure to rain," retorted Gertrude drearily. "And I hate going up the river."

"You don't generally," said Catherine, smiling. "What is the matter, dear?" she added, coming to sit beside her. "Are you angry with us?" Gertrude did not appear to be angry: she felt no clouding emotions; she saw everything with a dull, prosaic clearness.

"No," she replied brusquely to Catherine, "I didn't ask for anything," and she fretted her forehead against the cushions and rumpled the antimacassars.

"In that case," said her sister, with a gentle dignity, "you might do what we – what is the matter, Gertrude?"

Gertrude had turned at a small noise, and felt a white paw touch her cheek, followed by a mew. She let Robert Ellesmere slip to her, dropt her head over him onto the cushions; his fur was overwhelmed with a chaos of rich red hair, and the silence of the room was broken with the sound of a sudden and extraordinary burst of crying. Catherine left the room wondering, and the heart-broken sounds still recurred.

Book Two

Chapter 1

Mr. Valentine Amiens

In a generally red and brown, artistic dining-room in the west end of London two young men in evening dress sat stirring their coffee. One of them showed an evening equipment shiny with every fad of fashion, reminding one of an invention with all the latest improvements: one of the latest of all being a light screw of moustache. But despite this tuft of consummation, and despite the general varnish and curtailment given by the interval of six full and giddy years, it was Lucien Fleury that sat there, chirping out his latest eternal passion or incomparable pony to his companion opposite. His companion was a slim, dark, languid young man, with a youthful oval face and a quaint setting of his dark eyes that gave him that half-Chinese look that some French lads exhibit. He was Lucien's cousin from France, Valentine Amiens, who was, however, in many respects as English by habits and opinions as any Englishman that despised everything he didn't know. Lucien had seen very little of him previously, though he had some acquaintance with him and his sisters at the seaside many years before; but he remembered them as sweet-tempered and pure-minded people, and the two qualities looked out, with whatever listlessness, from the dark eyes of the young guest.

"Did you say you had met those young ladies before?" Lucien was saying, as he took another lump of sugar for his coffee.

"Yes," said Valentine, arching his eyebrows. "Oddly enough, I met them accidentally long ago, at the same time as I first met you. I don't know whether you remember it at all: it was once when we were all down at the sea-side, five or six years ago. They were kind enough to ask me to a party: and I danced with one of them, the eldest, sufficiently to make her almost as shy and awkward as I was. There was a very odd character there, I remember, who made me laugh rather. I never thought I should come on them again. What good people they seem to be."

"Oh rather!" drawled Lucien admiringly. "Oh yes ... I flatter myself they're as good girls as you'd find," he murmured with an air of speaking of something he'd "picked up" cheap.

"Good girls are much easier to find than good boys," said Valentine with his hands in his pockets. "A boy generally has good in him, but a girl somehow can be good all through. I wish I could express myself better. Those girls blow through one and do one good somehow. We have exchanged lances for umbrellas in this age – but sometimes – at any rate there is more satisfaction in admiring a family of brave good women, for it shows one can know them without the miserable sniggering folly of flirtation. Those seem to me to be the sort of women that changed men – and made men do things." Like most other poets, to which class he belonged, Valentine had a slovenly way of expressing himself in ordinary life.

Lucien listened to his words with a slight ruffling of his conceptions. He screwed up his eyes with a smile of faint demurring. "Of course, you know," he said with a laugh, "they're good, you know ... very good girls ... but they're not ... not exactly as distinguished as that ... not the kind of women you and I meet in the world, not like the splendid women. You mustn't expect them to be a bit dashing; so to speak. They're very good.... They stop at home too much for your idea; and are fond of each other and all that. Of course I like them very much, you know, but when I want influence ... why then it's different." He finished off with the same happy little laugh and sipped his coffee.

Valentine sat playing with his tea spoon. "I was thinking about the Athenians," he said.

Lucien broke into another crowing laugh. "What were you doing that for?" he enquired, beaming.

Valentine appeared to collect himself before replying. "The Athenians, it is reported, treated the female sex upon the true democratic principle of a division of labour. They selected as wives decent and hard-working women and called them by one name which I forget. They then locked them in a kind of everlasting kitchen and told them to do the housekeeping. Then they had another set of women, about whom the less said the better, and called them another name I forget. These women were very clever and amusing and said all sorts of funny things. They also dressed well, I believe. So you see the enlightened Athenians went to the bad women when they wanted wit, and went to the good ones when they wanted dinner."

"Well, and what then?" asked Lucien, somewhat bewildered.

"Oh, nothing," said Valentine lazily. "But Athens was the mother of civilization. We owe a great deal to Athens."

"But what do you mean, my good fellow?" said Lucien, beginning to think that genius was to madness near allied.

"Nothing particular," said Valentine, a red spark rising in his pale cheek, "only this ... we are a good deal too Athenian in our method with women. The *Alruna wives*[1] of our teutonic ancestors and the mothers in Israel of Semitic moralism were alike in this that they were great through goodness: and the combination of the two produced the Queen of Love and Beauty of mediaeval chivalry. But the curse of our modern man of the worldism is that we court the women we disapprove and despise the women we respect: we talk of a good woman lightly, like an old household chattel, and forget that her price is above rubies. We are not lowest on our knees before the pure and tender woman, but before two eyes and half a dozen diamonds. I am sick of all this *fin de siècle* sniggering over wit and culture and the rest of it. Did wit bring us into the world? Did culture bear pain that we might live? Did they love us in our silly fractious childhood and have no thought on earth but us? Can they comfort us, or kindle or sustain? Do we go to an authoress when we are wretched, or think of a woman of fashion when we are tempted? No, indeed: beauty is deceitful, and favour is vain: but a woman that feareth the Lord she shall be praised: give her the portion that is due to her, and let her works praise her in the gates!"

Valentine Amiens had risen to his feet and his head was thrown up, and his dark eyes impassioned, as he spoke: and Lucien, most convincible of human beings upon the abstract points, gave up his point easily.

1.- Alruna wives are household goddesses in Scandinavian mythology.

"Shall we join the ladies?" he said, laughing. "You are uncommonly eloquent, old man," he added as they moved towards the drawing room. "What's the meaning of this tirade to the glory of good women?"

Valentine did not answer but opened the door of the drawing-room to enter, where Catherine Grey, dark-haired and womanly, stood warming one restless foot upon the brass fender.

Chapter 2

In the Drawing-Room

When they passed out of the red-brown artistic dining-room into the blue-green artistic drawing-room of Mr. Fleury's house, they found the ladies to some extent impatient for them. The ladies were three in number, besides Lucien's sister, Cécile, a dark, very beautiful girl. We have known them before, but that was many years previously, when they were almost children.

Catherine the eldest was tall and impressive, still of the same full type, and broad, open, serious features: her dark hair was bound up in one massy coil, and her dark violet eyes had the old wistful, restless look of ceaseless responsibility. Her face, though still of the wide, childish, almost Japanese type that harmonised with her broad figure, was worn a little paler than ever, but it still wore the half-defiant calm of unflinching sacrifice and resolution, of unbreakable sympathy and power. Her pale cheek blushed a little as the two young men entered the room, and she spoke with a very quiet voice. Her sister Margaret was an even more broad and cushion-like type of girl, with humorous grey eyes and an affectionate smile that belied them. She was lolling in an armchair, turning over the leaves of a decorative picture-book by Walter Crane, and she shoved it idly away to exchange a few laughing enquiries with Lucien. The third girl, Gertrude, was lithe, close-knit and peaceful, perhaps the most picturesque though not the most womanly and attractive, with a low aureole of auburn hair, a dash of mischief in her eyes, but a rather tired smile on her full lips. All three were in dark green dresses, very quietly artistic.

"What have you been talking about all this time?" asked Margaret. "Has Mr. Amiens been reading you his last tragedy in twelve acts?"

"Not quite that," said Lucien with his honest, pleasant superficial laugh, "but you've no idea what I've had. Oh - he's been lecturing me all about lances and lady-loves and mediaeval chivalry and I don't know what all.... I promise you there wasn't much left of me."

Catherine looked at Valentine who looked at the ground and smiled dreamily, perhaps a little vainly. "Perhaps Mr. Amiens will lecture us," she said almost timidly, and Valentine coloured like a girl.

"If you had lived in the latter end of the 13th Century, Mr. Amiens, what course would you have pursued?" asked Gertrude, the mischief showing in her feline eyes.

"Prayed to get into another one," said Margaret, yawning, "that's what I should have done. Do you think it was an agreeable time, Mr. Amiens?"

"Well ... yes, I do," said Valentine, with the languidly indifferent utterance with which he invariably and involuntarily began his words, however he warmed up to them afterwards. "I think it was a time with a good deal in it – I wish I could explain how. It was a time when men weren't hag-ridden by logic, but thought in images: the quaint gambols and delusions of courtly life, for instance, were embodied in Robin Goodfellow, just as the spiritual passions for which we have such very long words gleamed in every knight's dreams as the burning blood of the Holy

Grail. I don't say there weren't bad men, but the world was made of bad men and good men, not of pessimists and optimists and altruists and individualists, as we divide this chattering world nowadays. Every knight, bad or good, knew there was a code there to live up to, and went and did something, instead of thinking it his first business to make a code for himself and do nothing..."

Catherine's eyes had a light in their depths as she listened, but Gertrude's voice came clear and sudden and cheerful. "What I like about the Middle Ages was their excellent management of the family question. You see, about once a month, they had a great tournament in which all the males of your family joined, and if you were a lady you went and looked at them out of a sort of wooden box. Well, all these relations fought each other, and some of them were sure to be killed. The advantage is obvious. By this means they made a clearance of relations once a month; thus preventing that undue increase of relatives which I take to be the true root of pessimism in this much-abused 19th Century." Gertrude here laid her chestnut-haired head back on her chair and stared placidly at the ceiling. Catherine's brow clouded.

"Of course," resumed Valentine, a little embarrassed, "there are lots to be made game of in the tilting and head-cracking of the chivalry ages: but," and the flush came which always betrayed a stirring thought, "but in that too those poor barbarous iron-heads have one thing to say beside your precious civilizations, ancient and modern."

"Oh, don't mention it," said Gertrude, casually, "they're not my civilizations."

"I mean," went on Valentine, earnestly, "that the

ancient and modern civilizations perhaps take something else instead. For in the matter of deadly fighting (and no one was ever less drawn to it than I am), those old gothic nobles, knights, gentlemen at least did it themselves: they went down and took their lives in their hands, rulers as they were, and got their silly brains knocked out, prince and peer. They didn't force wretched convicts and prisoners to chop each other up in a circus, while they sat as curled and scented as ladies; they didn't make a grinning ring round a couple of poor brutal negro pugilists and take odds on hateful blows they would never face themselves: we have outgrown those high-born old maniacs that rushed on each other's spears shouting their lady's name: we go sniggering down to prize fights – "

"Only occasionally," said Gertrude, turning her mocking face to him, "my attendance at a prize fight."

"Gertrude!" said Catherine, and her voice rang through the room. Then she added softly, her eye-lids troubled with a sort of emotion: "I think Mr. Amiens is quite right about the old times."

Gertrude looked at her sister with a tender, cynical, inexplicable look. Valentine always found something unintelligible about the lively girl.

It can hardly be said that Catherine had ever previously shown any sight of this devotion to mediaeval usage. She had, I should say, possessed all the vague school-room theory about superstition and the murder of sovereigns in the Tower, which exists in most other British Philistines, to which Catherine's family, like a large majority of other noble, generous and indispensable people, undoubtedly belonged. The reason why she spoke so, whatever it was, was twinkling oddly in Gertrude's sharp eyes.

"Oh I have very little doubt Mr. Amiens knows all about the old times," she said, shaking her head and laughing. "Meanwhile, permit me to know a little about the new times. They may not be romantic, gentlemen may not tie themselves up in iron, nor ladies be regaled with a graceful tribute of periodical corpses, but the young man of the present day has his advantages. He is quieter: he washes more regularly: he knows rather more geography and arithmetic: and his temper is generally less glorious and more reliable. I am a child of a degenerate century, I fear: I like steam-boats and hansom cabs and partners in white kid gloves. I shouldn't like to change them."

"One would rather love or trust or marry a man who would fight for you," said Catherine, tossing up her head, a little flushed.

"Oh yes," said Gertrude, laughing immoderately at something. "But I assure you I never felt drawn towards any of the white kid gloves in that aspect. When I marry, I promise you it shall be in the 13th Century."

Valentine, but for the interposition of Catherine, would have been a little bit nettled: for though not proud, he was filled and exalted with his own conceptions of the world, and this note of satire jarred on him. But when Catherine so gently came to his rescue, he had something else to think of. Looking at the ground, as he always did when pulling himself together to speak, he said: "Of course, I always know there must be two sides to a question," (which he never did) "but what I mean is this. The classic civilizations, which people exalt and imitate now were, under whatever varnish of politeness, worshippers of force: force of muscle; of intellect; of numbers; of wealth; of persuasion. In proportion as a man was powerful in any way, he was admired. Individualism existed for the able individual, no-one ever dreamt of regarding the poor and unsuccessful as individuals. The strong man and the aggregate, the hero and the many, these were the elements of the old worldly civilizations. Into mediaeval history, under whatever stains and confusions, another element had entered, the worship of the weak, as such. I need not tell you where I think that element came from," his lip trembled a little, "or remind you whose symbol, the symbol of sorrow, simplicity and sacrifice, the crusader wore on his shoulder: or of the simple old hearts that beat high when they thought of the weakest and most beautiful of sights, a mother and child. And the centre of all this conception, the centre of their very lives, was the respect paid to woman, the weaker sex, which might have been scourged and enslaved by those hard-headed, hard-fisted old barbarians that set it on so fantastic a pedestal. The worship of goodness in woman was the centre of mediaeval ideals: I do not think it can be said to be the centre of ours; but at the same time I am prepared to allow something in Miss Grey's defence of the modern young man. God forbid that I should think a man cannot be chivalrous today, or that romance lies in pennons and morions wherever there are men in Israel who have not bowed the knee to Baal: wherever there is a sweet and wise woman, old or young, there will the eternal human heart ride forth like Sir Galahad. A young man today, in this whirling social cosmos, chased by sins, fretted by doubts, has still one sight which God sends him eternally; the sight which Adam saw when he awoke from sleep."

There was silence, and then Margaret stirred, her eyes bright with tears, almost for the first time in the life of that languid embodiment of common sense. Catherine stood with her fingers knotted, and her face as white as ashes; the eyes burning out of it. Then she became suddenly aware that Valentine had his eyes on her as he spoke, and the blood rushed up to the roots of her dark hair. Her sisters hardly supposed that the worn, pale house-keeper could have looked so beautiful. Gertrude was sitting bolt upright on the sofa: the tired smile still on her lips, and her eyes gleaming with humour, approbation, real kindness, though dashed with the irrepressible laugh. She looked at Valentine as if she really liked his ways and thought him a good fellow, but something in her very attitude seemed to say that she did not share her sisters' utter submission.

"I really don't wonder Lucien stopped long over his coffee," she said, brushing back her hair.

"I must really be going now," said Valentine, again a little embarrassed. "I have been troubling you too long."

"Not at all," said Catherine, recovering her social manners, abruptly. "I hope you will come again."

He bowed himself out and was gone.

"I like that fellow very much," said Margaret, looking at the fire. "He has such healthy ideas about things."

"Oh yes," said Lucien, genially, just as he had spoken of them. "Oh yes ... he's as good a chap as you'd find."

"Don't you think – don't you think," said Gertrude, screwing up her eyes humorously. "Don't you think a little, you know, haw, haw, don't you know?"

"Affected you mean?" said Margaret, indifferently. "He may be a little positive about his side of the question, but it is the only fault."

"He may be positive," said Catherine in a high trembling voice, "but he is positive about the right and truth of everything. He affects nothing but what he has, honesty and courtesy and high thoughts about everything. He is not a bit affected in the bad sense ... not a scrap." And her voice broke a little, for Catherine, not having had many emotions, had never learnt to conceal them.

"I never said that, dear," said Gertrude, quite kindly, but with an indescribable note of reserved insight, like a grown up person pacifying a child. "I only meant he was positive."

"Oh well," said Margaret, tolerantly, "human nature! Did you ever meet a person who wasn't positive, Gertrude, or who didn't talk about his own ideas."

Gertrude went and looked out of the window.

Chapter 3

Gertrude

Gertrude was now decidedly the beauty of the family. Her hair, red and radiant, and her features odd, frank and interesting, seemed to combine to form a type defiant of canons, but peculiarly unique and fascinating. She had a free, alert manner, and considerable conversational powers, of a light rattling kind, and with these qualities it need hardly be said that she was a good deal in request. All the friends that knew and liked her family regarded her as "the lively one", and were pleased to have her to anything. Lucien Fleury, who regarded the girls as his own property and ran them like a show, considered Gertrude by far his best performer. Catherine was sensible and invaluable for management, Margaret had a great deal of humour and reading when once drawn into conversation: Gertrude might be counted on always; she would talk to anybody about anything. You would always find her in one corner of a room or another, surrounded by friends and chattering away like a magpie. And yet there hung in everyone's mind, as it had hung in Valentine's, the impression that she was lives older than her sisters.

For the first three weeks that Valentine had known Gertrude she seemed to him perfect in her way, a child of sunlight, with her bright green eyes, flickering lips and irrepressible humour. After three weeks he began to feel as if he never got any further: as if she never showed him anything but her sunny ball-room manner.

She was perfectly natural, but everyone who knew her long came at last to that feeling. They never got any further into Gertrude. Some concluded that there was nothing in her but animal spirits, others that there was something that eluded them. Valentine Amiens, being a visionary, was not a practised reader of human nature and his mind vacillated between the two superstitions.

How far we may here pierce under this mystifying hardness that lay under Gertrude's social enjoyment, I am in doubt. One or two short indications shall fill a short and "ticklish" chapter.

One morning, one of the hundreds of mornings of those five years of her life, Gertrude came down to breakfast very pale, and the look of one who had been crying. All through the morning she was like one under a shadow: towards evening it wore off, and next morning she laughed and rampaged over that meal as much as usual. That night she seems to have had a dream; she had a singular habit of grotesque imaginative dreams, her nightmares as a child having been like those of a maniac. But that night Gertrude had had an old nocturnal sensation. She seemed to be crawling over sloping roofs of tiles at night and beside her a figure, and that figure was an atmosphere rather than a person: an atmosphere of Basil Howe. "You see," he said to her, "it is a good specimen of the tiler's art after all. Every one of these tiles is in its place."

"I am so glad," she had said, with tears of happiness, thrilled and heated as she was under the old powerful presence. He answered something forgotten, and the sensation faded. A vague half-forgotten glimpse of riding behind him on a piebald horse; and there she lay awake, the darkly glowing reality of the dream still clinging round her. As she came to herself slowly, she grew slowly saddened, and when she realised that it was a dream she was totally and literally heart-broken. No one who has not had a dream of the kind will understand.

Some times she indulged timorously in wild visions of some day meeting him again: of saying this and that to him, and renewing the brave old friendship of those far-off days. Then she grew so wretched that she hastily thrust away the memory and took a vow against it, growing harder and more cheerful as she moved away. She sought and found refuge in an affection for her sisters, not a very passionate one perhaps, but her whole husk of life was growing bright, light and dry.

One feeling only besides this remained. She liked any society, and talked with the "white kid gloves" in which she classified the male sex, with the fearless rationality of her family, but if there came in any way into the life of her family a young man of whatever talents and virtues, her attitude was instinctively hostile, more so in proportion as he was liked by her sisters. She did not seem to hate them, so much as to be angry at their existence, to depreciate them in comparison with some hidden standard. It was no wonder that the mystified young men of her acquaintance could not touch the sensitive, vibrating chord in this stiff, springy mind, for she hardly ever touched it herself. She always suggested one who had buried her soul somewhere and whose body was out on a frisk.

Just now, however, she felt, half unconsciously, that the dead thing was stirring in its grave. And the form that the sensation took was a vague half-envy of Catherine, in whose worn, womanly but eternally child-like heart was growing the dreamy dawn which is the light of youth.

Chapter 4

The Emotions of a Quadrille

The twenty-first of November was the day of Lucien Fleury's great party, and all his relations, of whom there were hordes, French and English and cosmopolitan, assembled in his large apartments, to go through the solemn fakir ritual with which the modern world honours the shrine of fellowship. Most of them, in an interval after the first dance, were standing about in groups, but one of them was walking rather conspicuously alone. He was a dark dreamy young man in an evening dress easy but unpicturesque, who looked about him with something of the shyness and embarrassment of a recluse. Valentine Amiens, for it was that gentleman, gazed bewilderedly round for some moments, and then seemed to see something that rivetted his attention, first with pleasure and then with surprise. As he walked to the entertainment he had thought of nothing but Catherine Grey. He had pictured to himself the quiet, dove-like maiden of the honest home: and looked forward to meeting her, to worshipping her and bearing her proudly amid all the worldlings of the land of fashion which Lucien affected. These were his thoughts as he paced the polished floors, when he looked up and caught sight of Catherine. She was in the thickest of the talkers, superb in a white feathery evening robe, and talking to a strange man and girl with the spontaneity of a woman of the world. Valentine contrasted the open-faced mistress of the fireside he had known previously with that white imperial figure and felt a little puzzled. Gradually, he began to grasp that he, like so many men, had had a vague conventional idea of the work of women, that he had forgotten that their duty of being sociable and fashionable is the most trying of all their duties, and that Catherine as she stood there placid and radiant in her white plumes and draperies, was working as hard and honestly at a traditional duty of modern women, as if she had been making any number of puddings. He felt this mistake of his, and was all the better for it, for in the case of so just-feeling and fearless a gentleman we need not mind saying that he had weakness of moral ostentation; an instinct of doing things with a flourish. He walked up to the group and presented himself to Catherine. She gave a slight start at his voice and then saluted him civilly, making some remark about the heat of the room. Valentine would not have noticed it if the room had been as hot as Calcutta or as cold as Spitzbergen, for he noticed nothing, but he assented abstractedly, and the strange man and lady moving off at this point, Valentine had Catherine to himself.

"Are your sisters here?" was Valentine's first question, not because he wanted them, but because of that habit of considering them collectively which we have noticed before.

"They are over there, I believe," said Catherine, indicating the middle of the room with her fan, "but I am not quite sure. I really can't keep them in sight, half the time." She uttered the words wearily, as if she had tried very hard, as she generally did.

"They ought to be grateful to you," was all that Valentine could think of saying, but he meant it.

"I am not so unreasonable as to ask for that," said

Catherine, smiling. "They think me a great nuisance, I expect. So would everyone else that hadn't had to be responsible for two children, for they are nothing else."

"Not everyone," said Valentine, very gently.

Catherine dropt her eyes and seemed troubled. At this moment Lucien darted up, shining from his teeth to his finger nails. "Oh Valentine," he said, with gleeful confidence, "will you dance a quadrille?"

"Will Miss Grey give me the pleasure?" said Valentine with unusual presence of mind.

Catherine took his arm with confidence and they advanced to the middle of the room, Valentine looking as proud as Lucifer, but not of himself. Lucien, having made up all the other couples, hopped up to Gertrude who was talking to an old uncle, and bore her off. I rather think he was in love with Gertrude then, but I am not sure. If he was not, she was his confidante as to the adorable beauty of somebody else. However this might be, Gertrude was not displeased, for she had an odd sort of superficial liking for Lucien: he was the neat embodiment of all that her lighter self now liked, fashion, good waltzing and good temper; but her liking had always the peculiar grown-up attitude, and Lucien, accustomed to the experiences of a "man" could not understand why this red-haired slip of a girl should patronise him like a boy.

Valentine stood side by side with Catherine, as the couples gathered and filled up the square, but he noticed them no more than flies. His eyes, like the gladiator's, were with his heart, and that was not so particularly far away.

"I don't suppose you remember," he said to her with a proud shyness, "but this is not the first time I have had this pleasure. I once danced with you down in the country when I was quite a boy; and I made a fearful fool of myself."

"I don't think so," said Catherine, her dark eyes shining a little. "I remember you trod on a little boy's toe, but you were very gentle with him afterwards, and he soon forgot it. One remembers little things, long ago, somehow."

"Some things," said Valentine in a low voice. He thought of the resolute, frank-eyed, child-managing girl who had guided and protected him as a shy schoolboy at that old party, and his simple heart went out to the brave useful woman, the same and not the same, with feelings it is difficult to analyse. Honest the retrospect was, but not vivid or indispensable, a light sentimental memory thrown in to complete the new misty poem of a very misty poetic consciousness.

"Well," he said with a mournful cheerfulness rather showily assumed, "you need not grudge me this one little dance for my happiness, for I promise you will not seek for many more when it is over. I expect I am about the worst dancer in the room."

Valentine was not haughty, but the last self-depreciation was said with a certain haughtiness, for he despised fashionable and non-intellectual accomplishments.

"I do not think of nothing but good dancing," said Catherine, spiritedly. "You may not be a good dancer, but I would sooner -" Here she stopped, reddened and blinked her eyes a little.

"Miss Grey," said Valentine, with his brain suddenly on fire, but his words were beaten down by the first clang of the dance music, and as they looked to see if their turn was come, they became simultaneously aware of Gertrude's watchful eyes which had been upon them all the time, with their palest green of excitement.

The next moment they were in the mazes of the first figure. Valentine, whose thoughts were in a new whirl, forgot the little dancing he knew and was piloted through by Catherine in a state of helplessness.

"How jolly this dancing is," said Gertrude across Lucien to Catherine, while Valentine was doing the *cavalier seul*, or rather, as it seemed to him, walking aimlessly backwards and forwards till he was given back his partner. Catherine did not answer, but she knew that in Gertrude's words the dance was a hint not to be befooled by the partner: and felt very indignant. "I don't really care for this much," said she to Valentine, "and there are two people ready to take our place. Shall we go and sit down?"

"I shall be only too glad," said Valentine, his wild state of mind rising higher and higher. To waste another moment on a paltry dance for a paltry civility at this supreme moment of his new life and passion was to him impossible. He stumbled after her to a seat in the corner of the room. Gertrude chafed fiercely at the blunder she had made. In the hasty refitting of the square, by which she shifted to one of the sides, she did not glance at who else had come up, but followed the two with her eyes, maddened, puzzled and powerless. Flippant as she was, she had permitted to grow up an immense family pride in her sisters, in their collective happiness, affection, sacredness from all tampering touch. And now had come this vapouring poet to break up the Eden, and for no adducible reason whatever she distrusted him. Yet she could not deny, after what she had seen and known of him, that he was innocent, honourable, capable of the very highest conceptions, capable perhaps of making a good girl very happy. She bit her lip with vexation to think that she not only could not be any use, but could not even come to a definite opinion as to the proper attitude to take towards the romance that was going on under her nose. She would have given worlds, even new dresses, for one common sense friend to consult with her and balance or ratify her solitary impressions; but she never made friends now. Margaret was the most rational person, but she hated responsibility: for one of the rare times in these mocking, giddy years Gertrude felt her own loneliness and emptiness. The music clove into her thoughts and she was obliged to withdraw reluctantly her burning eyes from the corner where her sister and Valentine were talking earnestly: she turned them wearily to her own *vis ą vis*, and the room suddenly swam before her.

She was right again in a moment, and an outsider would not have seen anything peculiar. Only an ugly little old maid and a partner who had to bend patiently down to talk to her, a spare, stately figure, a narrow white shirt-front, a bronzed keen face: the same, still the same, if it had been after a thousand years he never would have looked any different.

"Sides!" called out Lucien, excitedly marking time in his boyish love of music and dancing. And with the crashes of dance tunes, with face stricken white of a sudden, and heart battering as if it were beating down the walls where she had buried it, Gertrude Grey advanced to meet Basil Howe again after five long years. He advanced, according to the canon, bowed and retired with his partner. She was staggered for a moment, and then remembered, with a kind of deep exultant swell of laughter, tears and pride, how utterly like him it was not to make a scene during the dance, to figure solemnly through the idiotic squares and couples at this terrible and crucial moment. No flattering passion such as Valentine had shown, no virtue or action though the noblest in the history of the world could have made her heart leap so much as it did at one odd thing that was "like him".

Round went the whirl of conventional movements, now Gertrude found herself spinning on the arm of Lucien, now taking Basil's hand for a moment in the tramp of the lady's chain, and still her heart rose higher amid the pealing, senseless music, and the wild ecstasy, spirituality, absurdity of their silently stalking to and fro and bobbing up and down and never showing a watch-light of their burning hearts until the carnival was over.

The music boomed at last to a close, the groups broke up and two people simultaneously left theirs and met in the middle of the room. Howe took the two hands she gave him, looked at her painfully, then looked slightly away and gave them a hard little shake. The bright colour had come back into her face: it was quite enough: she felt as if they were back again years ago by the last stile in the fields above the sea, where she had last held that gaunt brown hand and looked into those sad grey eyes.

"You can be introduced to me if you like," were his first words, "and have another quadrille."

"No ... no," she said, laughing with a hysterical catch in her breath. "Let's go somewhere, Mr. Howe, and sit down – and talk."

"With pleasure," he replied, with his old promptitude. "I'll sit down and you shall talk. Where shall we go?"

"To the conservatory?" she asked with a shy smile.

"Strike home, strike home!" he groaned. "I have deserved this." He led the way to the conservatory, picking up somebody's fan with an insane comment, and exchanging a word with several neglected people he had danced with. Gertrude's face wore a smile and her eyes a bright far-off look. Howe reached the conservatory in a few strides, and pushed open the door. But just beneath him, on the first cushioned sofa of this green retreat sat two people. One he recognised as Catherine, a red flame in her cheek and her hands half breaking her fan, and the other was a slim narrow young man, with dark eyes kindled, bending to her. He looked at them a second with his walnut face oddly puckered, and then turned and looked at Gertrude enquiringly.

Chapter 5

In Which Three Unromantic People Hold a Council of War

Gertrude read his eyes easily, knew what he had seen, what he was thinking and why he hesitated to speak.

"Mr. Howe," she said, almost in a whisper, "that is why I wanted you so much. My sister is half in love, and I cannot see my cue. Not that," she added, fearful of his own personal sensitiveness, "not that that was all the reason why I wanted you. I have been wanting you, consciously or otherwise, for five years."

A knot appeared in his forehead that looked like pain, but which she knew by experience was only embarrassed pleasure. All he said, however, was: "Is the fellow up the same tree?"

"I think he is in love with her now: but I know so little of him: he is a poet and I have a prejudice against poets. I want you to tell me what it is right to do."

"With pleasure," he replied. "If you had asked me to do it, it might have been different. But if we are to hold a council standing at the nearest river gate, we must put off our own confabulations, for there is one person who is indispensable. Where is your other sister?"

"Margaret?" said Gertrude. "She is over there with his sisters. I will find her. But I am sorry she has to be told: it will be a trouble for such a kind, easy-going sister." With these words Gertrude (Howe instinctively trying to assist, though he couldn't possibly) was off to speak to Margaret, who shortly disengaged herself from the adoring Misses Amiens to whom she was telling anecdotes and came towards the conservatory.

"Mr. Howe," she said, after looking at him for a moment with an amiable surprise. "It's a long time since we've seen you surely. Why have you sent this flaming herald" (pulling Gertrude's hair) "to wake me from sleep?"

"The angel that woke you from your flowery bed, Miss Grey," replied Howe, cautiously, "had better give her own celestial account of it herself."

"Let us come into the library," said Gertrude abruptly. In a few moments they were all round the table in that dusty twilight apartment.

"Margaret," began Gertrude, falteringly and casting about for how to break the news, "would you be surprised at anything Catherine did?"

"Not now," said Margaret with a smile, "since she has taken it into her head to fall head over heels in love."

"You knew it," said Gertrude, wild-eyed.

"Am I a mole?" replied Margaret, lazily.

"Well, we will not stray into zoology," said Howe hastily. "If Miss Grey knows, there's so much less to do. Now, Miss Grey, what do you think of him?"

Margaret blinked: "I never think anything particular of anybody and still less of Valentine Amiens, for when he is in company he does all the thinking for us. But he seems a very good fellow now, and certainly in love with Catherine. My only fear is –" and she paused sleepily to collect her words, for she was not used to dissecting people, "my only fear is that he is the kind of fellow who would be rather trying to live with: who'd want you to be always at high pressure. Catherine is several degrees higher than I am, but she is nothing to Amiens. Catherine is a good, clever girl though she is my sister, but wives when they are older would sometimes like something else besides mysticism and the Holy Grail over the poached eggs at breakfast: and high ideas are not always so good as high habits when you are choosing for life. Now Amiens would never go wrong like Burns and Shelley: that I would put my life on, but my fear is he would be a nuisance like Thomas Carlyle, and Catherine was not meant to be the housemaid of an egoist. I don't talk much about these things or about any things, but I occasionally take a turn at thinking about them. The world takes these thinkers and geniuses too much on their own flourish of trumpets, whimpers over their self-made troubles and excuses their inexcusable faults a great deal too much nowadays. Valentine is a good fellow, but he is not altogether cut out for the duties I think a genius owes like any other man. I would rather marry myself or any of my sisters to a strong-willed and simple-hearted man, a man who thought little of himself: a man who didn't mind pleasing others and mixing in the honest society fun of other people, than to all the Valentines rolled into one." Margaret concluded these last words of her plain and quiet statement with her usual composure, but Gertrude's eyes dimmed and her half-smile glimmered as if she found a new meaning in them. She looked at Howe and broke out:

"I think what Margaret says is truly right. For an honest woman of the world an honest man of the world is the highest union, you could not have anything higher. Poets are married to their ideas; if they want to marry in the other way, let them take quiet, stupid girls who will manage them properly and not try to enter into their thoughts. Catherine is too clever and not clever enough. Valentine would make her unhappy without meaning to. I never liked the idea, and now I think I see why."

"What do you think, Mr. Howe?" said Margaret.

Howe was staring at the table while they spoke, pulling his hair as he had a habit of doing and knitting his black eyebrows in thought. When he heard Margaret's voice, however, his face cleared to its usual social passiveness, and he said slowly and in a very unobtrusive voice: "I wish to preface all my remarks with a statement of my belief in the strong probability that you are right and the absolute certainty that I am wrong, an opinion deduced, if none of the others are, from long experience. Now I know very little of my cousin Valentine: I do know a little, though I studiously concealed the fact from you, not wishing to prejudice you unduly against him at the outset. But I am not going to talk about Valentine's psychology; he talks about that quite enough himself. All I have got to say is this, and it's very rude. Don't you think that you are choosing ideal wives and husbands for a lady and gentleman respectively when you might (if you were guided by me, of course, who am more than man) remember that they have done a little choosing for themselves? A pair of eyes twenty-two years old are not infallible guides to a life's partner, but they are likely to be more accurate (notice my old-fashioned courtesy) than somebody else's pair of eyes two years younger. And the choice of the first pair of eyes has this important advantage over the second pair, that those eyes stand a fair chance of seeing their choice the same to the end. They may be dimmed with tears (I believe that's the right expression) but they will still see something there that other people cannot see: and take an eccentric pleasure in it. And let me ask you, Miss Grey, how you think your sister would stand the easy transplanting of her feelings into this Dutch garden of an existence you suggest. The fact is, Miss Grey, I actually mean this in a sort of way, when I say that you will sow the same seeds that have led to many a broken and useless life such as I have seen in the world if you go on the principle that matches can be made, and matches broken off, and hearts banded about as if they were not hearts, as if logics and cautions and family councils can ever really touch the mysteries and maladies that only – I, of course, in reality understand and remedy. Briefly, I am not an infidel about this love: I am the merest, mildest, most meek and unoffending of agnostics. As to Valentine, I will not trumpet him. I came to marry Caesar not to praise him. But let me remind you of this. You see Valentine as a lofty, scornful faddist. There is one that sees him as generous and chivalrous, the King of men. Do you know which is right: do you know whether love or scepticism be insight? You cannot say that he is criminal, that he has anything of the murderer in him or even a *soupçon* of the burglar. Let that be enough for you: there is another that sees more (myself, of course, I mean). Hear ye then the conclusion of the whole matter. Trust the human heart: it is blind and blundering, but I fancy it is the best thing in stock. It flies straighter than our logic: to the last it is a reality. We *cannot* guide it: trust it. Let a woman leave father and mother (as Sydney Smith wittily observed) and take her chance like the rest of us. I am only twenty-three (slim, graceful and attractive) but I have seen a good deal of the world, and I feel if you keep love in you somehow, it will keep a kind of furnished apartments for you in the blackest lonely existence."

Margaret and Gertrude were both bent forward eagerly to listen to this strange speech, and there was something about its manner curiously stirring. The dry, self-restrained voice, the spasms of nonsense, the sudden excursions into the shape of his own didactic attitude, the tone of struggling thought and stifling pride that fought throughout it, contrasted harshly with the ringing declamations of Valentine; but there was far more in it also: the intense and burning sympathy for humanity, not the pale humanity of the poet but the motley struggling humanity of the man; the worn allegiance to affection, the real Christianity of his half-repressed references; all these, it must be admitted honestly, contrasted with Valentine also. Margaret only felt vaguely that he was broader, more human than she had supposed: but Gertrude, knowing him so well, followed every word with her heart rather than her ears, and when he had finished her stronghold of prejudice and rationality seemed a paltry cardhouse laid in ruins. She did not regret it, she did not hark back to his abuse of it; it was enough for her to think him more than right: divine. She gave up her point eagerly, and Margaret assented. Persons who understand Basil Howe will find no difficulty in believing that the moment his view prevailed, it was with the greatest difficulty they could persuade him he was right.

Chapter 6

In Which Fortunes are Told, and also Fairy Tales

Valentine Amiens was standing by the sofa in the conservatory alone; Catherine having just flown from him. Yet the rare flush was on his face, and his eyes were bright as they gazed into vacancy. Just then the door opened and Basil Howe entered silently.

"Basil!" cried Valentine, with a cordial smile at his grim cousin, and put out his hand. "I didn't know you were here."

"Nor did I," replied Basil, greeting him politely. "I rather thought I was dead and buried. Do you keep that muse of yours still?"

"A little," said Valentine with a gratified smile.

"I thought I heard you were suited," replied Basil. "I wish I kept a muse." Valentine laughed at the idea.

At this point the door again opened and Gertrude appeared. It was on this cautious principle that the conspirators adjourned to the conservatory.

"Oh, let me introduce you," said Valentine, rather gracefully. "Basil, this is my friend, Miss Grey: Miss Grey, Mr. Howe."

A mad prank signalled itself in Gertrude's eyes, as she swept a distant salutation to which Howe replied with a bow of terrific courtliness.

"I think I have heard of Mr. Howe," said Gertrude graciously. "You are the 'promising barrister', are you not?"

"Oh yes, constantly promising," replied Howe readily. "I am as you hint a barrister by profession in the more literal sense, but by practice, to break it gently, a journalist."

"So I had a kind of intuition," said Gertrude mysteriously. "Did you know I was a gypsy, Mr. Amiens?"

"I was unaware of the fact," said Valentine, laughing.

"I am, though," said Gertrude, throwing herself onto the sofa and putting her hands behind her head, "and I can tell fortunes. I could tell yours, Mr. Amiens, I could tell what you were thinking about when we came in.

Valentine looked rather guilty and said hastily: "You know me so well. Tell Mr. Howe's and I shall believe you and your nonsense."

Gertrude thrust out her chin, as she had a habit of doing, screwed up her eyes and subjected Howe to a long scrutiny at which Valentine laughed loudly, but which Basil himself bore with most solemn and unmoved countenance.

At last she began: "There's something about you, Mr. Howe, which suggests that you are a humorist, but that you don't appear to like being it. Conversation, eccentric; habits, methodical; manners, good but not soft; life, solitary; industry, remarkable."

"Upon my soul, you are not far off the mark," said Valentine, wondering.

"As a journalist," went on Gertrude, keenly, "you are highly versatile and valuable, but do not appear to be ambitious. You always hated being a barrister but took it up uncomplainingly on the desire of your father, whom you had very seldom seen. Your life for the last five years has been successful journalism, varied by occasional successes at the bar; which have not, however, brought you any large income. Your demeanour during those five years has been, especially towards the end, one of violent energy at your nocturnal profession, but people have often noticed in you fits of gloom for two or three days together."

"I begin to think I am dreaming," said Valentine, staring at her, "or that you are a witch really. It is a life of him."

"As for you personally," went on Gertrude, leaning forward with the almost forgotten wilfulness of childhood, "you would be much better and happier if you would believe that other people are charitable besides you. You fancy everyone laughs and despises, whereas it is possible to laugh and love. You do not wrong society, as some people do, by saying it cannot appreciate your fancies, but you wrong it deeply by saying it dislikes you ..."

"Enough, enough," said Howe, dramatically, but with a certain real earnestness under his tone. "There is a great deal too much of me in this conversation, as elsewhere. A slight *soupćon* of me in the social cosmos is just bearable, but anything like a whole human being made out of it nauseates naturally enough. There is a delicacy in these things."

"You must be a gypsy indeed, Miss Grey," said Valentine, still mystified. "How did you find out so much about Mr. Howe?"

"I expect she dogged my footsteps upon the approved principle of a Romany: and her doubtless outposts of her countrywomen prepared to inform her of my movements. As Mr. Rudyard Kipling said to me in his chatty way:

The white moth to the closing vine,
The bee to the opened clover,

And the gypsy blood to the gypsy blood
Ever the wide world over.
Ever the wide world over, lass,
Ever the trail held true,
Over the world and under the world
And back at the last to you."

The particularly dogged and monotonous tone in which the last verse was quoted made Gertrude feel certain of a personal interpretation. She thought how Valentine would have delivered such a reference and smiled.

At this moment the door opened and Margaret appeared, followed by Miss Amiens aged seven years, followed by Catherine.

"Mr. Howe!" she said, putting out her hand with the gentle, chastened manner that had become so much more common with her of late, "I didn't know you were here."

"So many people have said that to me now," said Howe, with a perplexed expression, "I shall begin at last to conclude that I can't be here after all. We have just been considering the case of one, Miss Gertrude Grey, who did on that occasion unlawfully use certain subtle means, to wit fortune telling to impose upon and delude certain of Her Majesty's subjects, to wit one Valentine Amiens, poet. Do you believe in palmistry?"

Howe only talked because there would be an awkward silence, with the two lovers face to face, and after Valentine on whom a light had broken when Catherine spoke, had made some embarrassed reply. The awkward silence set in. It was broken by the clear voice of Valentine's little sister, who addressed Margaret abruptly: "Tell me another fairy story." Everyone laughed in a relieved sort of way, and Margaret said, yawning, "Oh, I've forgotten all the rest. Ask Mr. Amiens to tell you one."

Valentine was staring out of the window, with drowsily burning eyes, and began with startling prompitude like the continuation of his own thoughts, "Once upon a time, there dwelt a King in fairy land" ("Impossible," said Howe in parenthesis) "who founded an order of holy knights. And they vowed not to drink nor hunt nor marry, nor do ought but meditate upon sacred things and go upon sacred quests. And there was one among these knights who had a dream in which he saw a white marble-like figure, as if of a young man like to himself beckoning him to follow. And when he awoke he told his dream to the priest, who said that it surely was of heaven, and proclaimed it from the house tops saying that one of the order had had a vision from on high. And the knight rode out into the dark woods to seek the image of his dream. For five years he rode passing through fields and shrines, roads, cities, universities, and thought of nought but it. And at last there came to the ears of the King a tale that told of how his knight had given up the search for the white youth and had stuck his spear in the ground and tethered his horse to a tree, and dwelt with a cottage maiden in a distant glen. And then all cried shame on him that he had given up the search for the white youth and wedded a woman, and the King and all his knights sallied out and sought him where he stood, tilling a little garden beside the sea, while his gentle wife sang at her spinning. And when the knight saw that the King and all his banners were drawing nigh, he took down his old helmet and spear and mounted his old horse and went out to meet them. And then the King said, 'What sayest thou, once my subject, who has sinned against the light?' And then the knight cried out in a clear voice, 'Nay, rather am I the one that by no merit of mine own have found it. Listen; for though our blood may soon be on each other's spears, it is well that truth be told. For five years I sought the white one and meditated upon it and on my privations and on my final glory in achievements, and one evening when my heart was heavy, I saw a maiden singing and working among the corn. And when I saw her face, the white figure seemed a shadow of myself, and she the sun of life. For how know I that the white self was assuredly of heaven; how know I he was not a proud dream come of the tempter; or a pale replica thrown on the darkness from disordered vanity. And even if the white self was at the time of heaven: he was but I, a bloodless tracing of myself in every feature: but this is another face, a face that is different, and, therefore I know that God hath sent it to me, to be the filling up of my life. This face that can blush and laugh and weep, this I know is of the Lord, for it has grown with his daisies beneath it and his apples above: this and no pale mirror face is what a man should seek. Therefore, if there be any man among you that dare say I do wrong, or that there is a fairer goal than my lady, him I challenge to the death with sword and spear, so help me God on high.' And even as he sat waiting in the saddle, the king turned his bridle rein, and all the host turned in silence and rode home. And as the knight went back and took off his helmet, his wife cried out, seeing that his face blazed like a star. And he turned aside and looked into a mirror pool and beheld the light and face of the white self, which had passed into him. Yet he did not vaunt it nor think of it, but turned only to his lady."

Valentine stopped as if a long stream of inspiration had passed; and sank quickly almost scornfully in his seat, his eyes still fixed on Catherine. "Tell us another," said the little girl, breathlessly, before anyone could utter their comment on the strange form and undercurrent of meaning in the fanciful story. Valentine laughed and said, with his shy laziness, "You're very exacting, Marjory. Ask Basil for one."

Marjory went up to that gentleman, who was leaning over the back of a chair, the red chinese lantern glistening on his sallow features and shiny shirt front. "Tell me a story, please," said the small petitioner. Basil Howe scrutinised the little black-headed imp with a curious mingled expression, for he knew her well, and was a great favourite with her and her little sisters, and then said to her with an obeisance due to a small duchess, "Your ladyship shall be obeyed. Know then that in the palace whereof the prophet Amiens has spoken there was a jester, who was kept there that his lunatic capers might make sport for the knights and give them a little mental relief from the stress of running after different coloured selves and having faces like stars, which is always a wearing occupation. And this poor jester had nothing to play with when by himself save a bauble, the top of which was adorned (as your profound historic knowledge will doubtless tell was commonly the case) with the fool's head, and this head was as like to the jester's own as the white vision was like to the knight, save that it was carved with an elvish grin, so that whenever the buffoon felt unhappy even to tears by himself, it was there before him laughing, to remind him of his duty to society. He did not tell this to a priest, because he was generally considered out of the pale of Christian tolerance; he told it at once to the butler, and the butler did not tell him that it was assuredly of heaven, but on the contrary related it to another part of the theological system. And so the jester moped about and cut capers," said Howe, bestriding a chair and drawing the child nearer to him with an obscure gentleness that surprised her brother, "and the only pleasure he had was occasionally to romp with the little village children on the green and make them laugh; because he thought that perhaps some of these had not learnt to despise him as half-witted. But whenever he thought of them, there was the buffoon face of himself as a professional reminder: his only companion. And he used to walk about in a costume which was red on one side and yellow on the other, for that was considered the wittiest thing possible by our simple forefathers: and he wore bells on his head like a donkey (to which indeed many of his friends caught a remarkable likeness) so that they rang wherever he was going, and anyone who didn't feel well or was depressed already, or wished to retain their youthful freshness of mind, fled at his approach. And one day as he was sitting alone on the steps, staring wistfully out of his old red hood, he heard a voice say to him, 'Why are you so unhappy, poor clown?' And he looked up and beheld a graceful and glorious princess who had wandered from her nursery. Then he fell down on his knees and told her everything: and she smiled compassionately and let him kiss her hand and passed on." Here Howe stopped a moment. "And what did the jester do next?" was the earnest question: but the voice was not Marjory's, but Gertrude's.

"Oh then the clown crawled back to his place on the steps and, taking his grinning bauble in his hand, said to it, 'Sir: you have grinned at me for twenty years, but now another smile has been smiled upon me. It will never smile on me again, I shall never see her again: but because she has thrown a word to me, I give my life to that one memory; and you, you devil, go.' And with that he dashed the bauble to pieces and hurled the haft into the sea. And then he limped off and entered the banquet hall walking on his hands, amid much applause."

The crash of the last waltz within finished off the odd story and drowned the stir of emotion and mystification it evoked. Almost before the audience were aware, Howe had risen and with a hurried general salutation had run off to take farewell of his host.

Valentine rose about the same time and fell apart to take a lingering farewell of Catherine. Gertrude and Howe had exchanged a look.

Chapter 7

The Poet and the Journalist

If ever the backs of two men could be almost as expressive as their faces, that was the case with the two young men whom Lucien saw depart from his lamplit hall that night. The languid manner and sloping shoulders of Valentine Amiens, his loose but aesthetic scarf fluttering at his throat and his long, poetic cloak flapping round his heels looked the embodiment of negligent dignity and contrasted oddly enough with the tight-braced, square-jointed, black-clad figure of the journalist, in which there seemed not an inch of dark cloth superfluous or awry. What was it then, in the face of the contrast between this bohemian untidiness and that iron neatness, that suggested that Valentine was the vainer of the two?

Basil Howe was not displeased that Valentine had a fancy for talking as they went home, for the diversion drew away his thoughts from himself, with which, as usual when he had at all come out of his shell, he was particularly dissatisfied. The shock of finding himself so suddenly and dizzily among the people who had been the one warm spot in his bleak life, and made him intensely emotional and even communicative, and now he thought, as usual, that he had been a bore.

Valentine talked, as he always did, profoundly and sincerely, and his theme was the one now invariable with him, the unspeakable sacredness and goodness of "some people": which Howe understood very well.

"Surely – " Valentine was saying with his flowing voice, "surely this is the great comfort: the great religion after all. The world is filled with silly noises, and senseless social forms, and endless gibbering and laughter: but there are some people in it who never hear the evil voices: who would be pure in the heart of hell. They are like the elect of God, they come onto the earth children of light: they dwell eternally in a light and atmosphere which they create, a heaven diffusing from them. People may talk as they like, but the old Hebrew was right: there is an eternal and vital solidity in the position of the righteous: Blessed is he that hath not walked in the council of the ungodly nor walked in the way of sinners, nor sat in the seat of the scornful. Think of – Miss Grey and then of Lucien and you will feel what I mean about the difference. Good people have really a strength about them: a rooted, real character, which one does not feel in the vicious and fashionable who are as chaff before the wind. These gentle queens and kings are crowned silently for ever: something, I know not what, does give them a sign, a freshness, the stamp of moral caste, amid all the yelling brutalities and buffooneries of modern complicated life. Would that we were back among the charities and chivalries of a simpler social existence."

"Social existence was no doubt greatly simplified by the charity and chivalry of poking holes in each other with long spears," replied Howe, the slightest bit abruptly. "I quite agree with you about the good people, though I can't express it so well, but I believe that all those perfect Middle Ages were the entire creation of the nineteenth century."

"But surely they were pure, more graceful?"

"Read Chaucer," said Howe dryly, "not these Tennysons and Rosettis that have built a Middle Ages of their own out of tapestries and fads and stained-glass windows. When our fancies are blurred with those *fin de siècle* phantoms, old Chaucer blows through one like an April wind. In Chaucer he and his age appear as what they were and ought to have been, more or less, a strong, varied, hopeful, vigorous, coarse society. There was quite as little charity and chivalry about the miller and the sumpnour as there is about any dandy in London: the other two had good in them of course, and so has the dandy. And what Chaucer's society was our society is, only his was rather worse, ruder and more bestial at any rate. And this is another difference, and the biggest of all, that Chaucer had faith in his society, and you poets will not allow us to have faith in ours. But why not: heaven forbid that I should criticise your poems. I may have to do that tomorrow night, with the copy to be made in ten minutes; but let me ask why we shouldn't have faith in this society?"

"The age of chivalry is passed," said Valentine, sadly.

"Not this evening, I think," said Howe, keenly. "Permit me to say with that old fashioned courtesy for which I am remarkable, that I don't believe a word of that statement. The mediaeval knights have the eternal honour of having introduced respect to women, but it is flatly untrue to say that they brought it to its best. Women are better treated now in every sense of the word, people think and expect more of them. You and I are aware of reasons for respecting them of which Bayard knew nothing whatever. Chivalry has increased, all the gentler virtues have increased with civilization: kindness to women, as much as kindness to children which, though it was laid down eighteen hundred years ago is almost newly understood, like a good many other observations made on the same occasion. I don't wish to refer any more to that painful subject, but does it not strike you that enlightenment is beginning to teach us to understand a historical character compounded of the chivalrous virtues, which must have remained a sealed book to the coarse Middle Ages? I believe we have a better idea of what is good than they did: I believe we try more."

"If I could think that I should look with more pleasure on the modern world," said Valentine, wrinkling his brow, "but I cannot see the good and beauty of this time but as a survival, a fading priesthood from a better time. Everywhere beauty is giving way to gigantic vulgarity, conduct to gigantic talk, faith to gigantic irreverence. Advertisement is everywhere: vulgarising of all old learnings and mysteries: cheapening of all secret and sacred things. Journalism, its voice the condensed bray of five hundred mob-meetings, its blazon the painted hoardings that are covering London with hideousness, its God the public, its prophet the penny-a-liner: Journalism stalks abroad gigantic and treads down sooner or later with its universal Ragnorake of equalisation all the old lamps of treasured knowledge, the delicate songs of dreamers and lovers: the starry and lovely epics of the old makers of the earth. Everywhere there storms in on us this all-conquering ugliness. What is it that we want?"

"Faith!" said Howe, with an emphasis that made Valentine jump at the word, especially when uttered by such an entire "actualist" as Howe. "Faith is what we want. The old makers didn't think about dead and buried times, they thought about their own. They had faith in God and therefore faith in chivalry, in monasticism, in wars, in pilgrimages, in dynasties. What we want is faith in God and therefore faith in science, in steam-engines, in county councils, in dock strikes, in journalism. Your Ragnorake idea would be well if it were Frigga or Odin we believed in, but why cannot God lay his foundations with these large, popular things as much as with the old rude, blood-thirsty things? It is all very well for you to talk about ugliness, but your talk is the merest aestheticism, it doesn't touch the moral wants of the people at all. A battle-axe may be a prettier thing than a steam-engine, but a steam-engine sends home hundreds of men every day safe to their wives and families: and the battle-axes only chopped up their heads. Why don't you write the epic of the steam-engine as Homer wrote the epic of the chariot? The men of Homer's time probably thought a chariot just as commonplace. It was only the seeing eye that saw its beauty in its use. For my part Whitman's 'Song of the Broad Axe' seems to me a long way the most heroic poem of this time."

"But surely," said Valentine, dubiously, "there is nothing really heroic in these things. They are all done for the million, comforts provided cheaply for the herd: information given to gratify their various forms of scandal-mongery and horror-mongery. Journalism is only pandering to the low aggregate intelligence, to the herd."

"Precisely," replied Howe, cheerfully, "though why it should be called pandering to the herd to provide the herd with its proper and healthy food, I don't know. And it's all very well," he said, warming a little, "for you to abuse journalism: it works pretty hard to provide honest literature every day for a penny to the masses that your poetry leaves as much in the dark as they were before, and that by the way is not so dark as you are in the habit of supposing. I know that literary men call it 'superficial', 'cheap'; it is one of the simplest ways of proving yourself expensive to say that. But I deny it: read the leader in a recognised paper on any subject literary, scientific, ethical: I defy you to say that it is not generally phenomenal in its power, knowledge and healthiness of tone. I have read articles in penny papers that would have made essays in a good many five shilling gentlemen's volumes, and I know how fast and at what terrible pressure those able bits of writing are produced. The world now lives at this pressure and on this collective principle, and journalism is the only literature which grapples bravely with the world as it is. Journalism is not cheap, it is not even light: it is simply intensely human: the life blood of our society."

"But this principle of publicity," said Valentine, knitting his brows, "everything now is getting public: the sweetest fireside secret and the most loathsome private infamy are alike dragged to light. Men of genius are dragged out in the noose of the interviewer to dance and make sport for the Philistines. Surely this asmodean madness: this staring in at each others' front windows, is a sign of the end."

"Publicity is another thing I always thought over-abused," replied Howe. "Why should people want to know things? There is nothing shameful in publicity as such, apart from the thing made public. Why shouldn't the public want to know about men of genius? There is nothing morally wrong in feeling an interest in what great men think and look like, and there is nothing morally wrong in satisfying such a want. Of course, if you choose to entertain a private aesthetic feeling against it, to that you have perfect right, but there is nothing moral in the feeling: and nothing immoral in the publicity, if the motive that prompts it is honest interest. You literary geniuses are too fond, I think, of scoffing at the large, human sociabilities and sentiments and curiosities of the masses when after all, these things are the evidence of their profound moral passions, their rude emotional love of the good and brave and romantic, like their applause at a noble sentiment in an Adelphi drama, one of the most refreshing sounds one can hear, I think. I believe in the masses. Out of them have come every moral movement in the history of the world: and not a single one out of the cultured class. That is why – but perhaps we will not enter into that. I do not know your politics, Valentine."

"Oh," said Valentine, laughing, "I am a Tory to the backbone."

"Ah, well then," replied Howe, "perhaps we had better avoid all discussion of our respective vertebrae."

They walked on for a little while in silence, and then Valentine spoke. "I can't help going back to my original thought: the good people. They are not the many, but they are the salt of the earth. The difference between these shining chosen ones and the herd makes me a Tory on my own lines. Don't you feel a difference somehow between Lucien and Miss Grey, that makes one believe in a noble few?"

"Heaven forbid that I should deny Miss Grey's right to be *regina et imperatrix* over all civilized nations," replied Howe, with an odd look at his cousin. "But as regards the herd, I can only go back to *my* original thought, if any of my observations can be described by that name, and say that I like herds: that I have an almost pastoral taste in them. I am one of the many myself, one of these very hop, skip and jump society worldlings whom you have held up to execration in the person of our cousin Lucien. But why be so down on him? He is nothing extraordinary, but there is the same good in him that there is in larger quantities in Miss Grey: and that good is mixed with various qualities in hundreds of these ordinary young men. He is not hard or cruel or underhand: why can't you take kindly that sort of people as they are and be glad of the good in them?"

"I fancy," said Valentine, half to himself, "I begin to feel that this was something of what Miss Gertrude Grey was trying to say, when I thought she was making game of me."

"Miss Gertrude Grey!" said Basil Howe and fell into a brown study. They walked on together a little further, and then Valentine spoke.

"Do you really think then that a weak, fashionable sprig like Lucien can come to good?"

"I would take a wager on it," said Howe, firmly. "Particularly if he could find someone to really like."

Valentine, coming at this point to his own garden gate, held out his hand, intellectually impressed, but spiritually entirely unconvinced. At the root of Howe's philosophy there lay a restless feeling, the source of Christianity, socialism and much else: a feeling of sympathy with the disregarded: of defiant protection of the simple, the aggregate, the anonymous. And the waves of this broad emotion beat in vain against Valentine's intellectual innocence, as against a high, cold, polished tower of ivory.

"Well, good-bye," said Howe, shaking hands, "I've

got to be off and vulgarise all sorts of things that have to be out tomorrow morning. Good night." And he vanished rapidly in the darkness.

Valentine's thought fled, like a loosened bird, back to another person, and Howe and his hopes were forgotten.

Chapter 8

The Garden of Eden

Early one morning, when the dew was just off the sunny lawns and bushes in the garden of the house of the Amiens family, a brown-beaked, hawk-faced young man in black clothes stalked hastily across the grass to where, just at the entrance of the shrubbery, a chestnut tressed young lady was standing, fretting with the keenest excitement.

"Are they in there?" enquired Basil Howe of the girl. Gertrude nodded, overbrimming with laughter, and added, "They will walk round the paths ahead of us, so we can go in there all right."

"So be it," replied Howe. "I will walk round with you after them like Mephistopheles after Faust and Margaret. You deserve a better part than Martha, but I will undertake to bear my rôle with all appropriateness." And indeed for the moment, with his long lean face and mocking accent, he would have done very well for Mephistopheles.

Meanwhile in the inner paths of the shrubbery another couple were standing, the girl fuller and more queenly, the young man slighter and more girlish-looking.

"Miss Grey," the young man was saying, "I asked you something the night before last at the party. You did not answer it wholly, but what you said encourages me to ask again. May I do so?"

"Mr. Amiens," replied Catherine, gently, "why need we talk about that?"

"We must talk about that," said Valentine, vehemently. "There is nothing else in the whole world to talk about. When I look up in the sky, the clouds are waiting for it: when I look down at the grass, the flowers are waiting for it. There is nothing now, nothing in the world for you or me, but that: shall I give it its name?"

"Let us wait a moment: let us walk on," said Catherine, looking up bravely, but with a troubled face: and they walked on.

"How much Lucien has improved," Gertrude was saying to Howe, as they walked abreast. "He seems to have quite turned over a new leaf."

"I fancy the other was only an ornamental title-page," said Howe. "I quite agree with you though. He is stronger and less morbid and generally reminds me less of a skeleton in plain clothes than he used to do: I have often thought by the way, that it would be a good idea if some enterprising member of my profession were to interview any of the principal ghosts and skeletons, those at the head of the profession, I mean, that do the haunting of the best families. Then in the dull season they might have a ghosts' strike: and a correspondent 'instantly on the spot': and of course an article 'Kensal Green Cemetery presented a scene of unwonted bustle and confusion, etc. etc. The whole scene was literally dead with ghosts, etc.' I believe I have the making of a most excellently conceited editor, and could run all sorts of paying ideas, if I could only turn over that new leaf you referred to now."

"I think you are turning over an old one now," said Gertrude, looking at him searchingly, as he covered his retreat with nonsense. "Why are you mocking so much now, just as you used to years ago. You don't seem to tell me what you think so much."

"Do you know what I think?" he said shyly, almost stubbornly. He was thrilled through to feel her reading him so keenly, for he had indeed been trying to re-assume their earliest relations. The first inflaming of his dark memories when thrown abruptly into her company had warmed him to involuntary tenderness; but now his steely conscientiousness had resumed sway, and he was saying to himself, "In a few years this good kind girl will fall in love and marry, and then the good man will only detest me for my anomalous attitude. Had I not better take myself out of her life as quietly and decently as possible.... At least I ought to, and I will try to want it." Outwardly, however, he only assumed the old light manner, which he judged the best line under the circumstances.

"You have something on your mind," said Gertrude, persistently.

"I am delighted to hear it," he replied. "If it stops there long enough, perhaps it might get inside."

Meanwhile Valentine had become again impatient of Catherine's long silence. They emerged at last onto a cleared space of daisied lawn, where a hawthorn tree overshadowed everything, and Valentine spoke.

"Miss Grey; I can wait no longer. In God's name tell me my fate."

Catherine hung her head like a lily and was still silent.

"Miss Grey," said Valentine, his eyes suddenly blazing, "Catherine – " and stopped.

Catherine made no sign and Valentine took her silently by the hand, for he had too much noble reverence to do more, and said, "Catherine, I have spoken and I think you have answered. Do not let me be deceived, for this is a question upon which any man has a right to have his answer: an hour that comes only once and must be taken as it comes. I do not think much of myself beside you, but I am an honest man, I can keep you with my pen and protect and labour for you always. Whatever the world gives to me shall be yours: nothing that the world can give will I ever value so much as you. Answer, Catherine, for this surely is the hour. Have you answered?"

Catherine lifted her head, heavy with the black Japanese coils of hair and looked fearlessly into his eyes. "Yes, Valentine," she said, and then the two drew together, and their faces were as those of two happy children.

"Oh yes, I know what a mathematician is," Howe was saying, "he's rather like a sort of small man. I had an uncle who was taken that way once. Dear me," he said, lifting the overgrown sprays of bramble away from Gertrude's head, "this is a very selfish rude tree; where are you going now?"

Gertrude escaped out through the briars, gazed a moment and came hastily back again. Howe, following the direction of her eyes through the thickets, saw under the hawthorn tree Valentine with Catherine, hand in hand.

"It is like the Garden of Eden," said Gertrude, almost with awe. "Thank you," replied Howe. "You offer me a second opportunity for appearing in my first rôle, in his more invertebrate form."

"Well," said Gertrude, laughing, "if you are the serpent, what am I?"

"I should be very sorry to say what you were, Miss Grey," said Howe seriously. "Perhaps you are Lilith, of Talmudic fame. As Rosetti said to me confidentially:

It was Lilith the wife of Adam,
(Eden's bower's in flower)
Not one drop of her blood was human,
Yet she was shaped like a soft sweet woman.
(O the Bower and the hour)."

"No, I don't think that is what we are," said Gertrude like one who had been following his words seriously.

"There is room for hope, I think," replied Howe, "that we may not after all be those persons: but you remember the poem and will excuse me. For my part, I always believed that those refrains with O's at the beginning of them, were really the remarks of Mrs. Rosetti expressing a true feminine contempt for Dante dear and his absurdities. 'O Troy Town!' and 'O Mother Mary, mother!' are exclamations of domestic remonstrance at his immersions in these subjects while the tea was getting strong. I think of publishing a book on the theory."

Gertrude spoke like one in a dream: "I cannot help thinking of the same thing again, the Garden of Eden. Adam and Eve in paradise. What is it makes me think that that is what they are: and that I am different: that we two are different."

"Perhaps you have been eating apples," said Howe dryly.

"Apples?" said Gertrude, whose scripture recollections were not so exact or extensive as Howe's. "... Oh yes, it was the tree ... what was it?"

"The tree of the knowledge of good and of evil," he replied.

A few weeks afterwards Valentine came up to Howe, with an air of embarrassed hilarity and told him he was going to be married, to which Howe replied with the required astonishment and was asked whether he would be the "best man".

"Not if you have many of them," replied he mysteriously, "but may I ask, I am aware it is irrelevant to the situation, if you know whom you are going to marry?"

"The eldest Miss Grey," he replied.

Howe put out his hand, "I congratulate you heartily: only don't let it occur again." And took himself off.

The marriage between Valentine Amiens, man of letters, and Catherine Grey was one which attracted considerable attention, for Valentine was a rising star in the literary horizon and several high cliques had taken him up. Many simpering and well-dressed persons with pince-nez and views came to patronise his wedding and his wife, with whom they were agreeably surprised, for women like Catherine can bear any light and any elevation.

Weird-looking intellectual ladies in art colours laughingly implored Valentine to show them all his love-poems: a request which, if he had acceded to it, would have obliged them to hire several waggons for the purposes of carriage. The speech of the best man (Mr. Basil Howe, known to them as the brilliant lieutenant of a distinguished editor) was generally considered the success of the wedding entertainment, and the same gentleman contrived to hold any number of regenerators of society conversationally at bay when the arrangements required it. Everybody drove away delighted with Valentine, Catherine and the marriage, for the world is not in the least cynical, but on the contrary the most sentimental of planets, and was quite proud of this genuine "match of inclination", which had been approached by the usual stages of time-honoured love-making. This was the history of the socially famous marriage of Miss Catherine Grey, and with it we may close her history. Of people like her one may predict a peaceful and honourable life.

Margaret was also married. She did not exactly have a romance, for there was not a scrap of that element in her composition: but she grew very honestly and genuinely fond of a young country gentleman, of a chirpy and charitable type, and after a few years married him, in a tolerating sort of way: and was rewarded with a slavish and life-long devotion, at which she laughed, but in which she took a very peaceful pleasure.

Chapter 9

The Confession of Gertrude Grey

Mr. Basil Howe stood outside the house of the Grey family, still under the charge of their aunt, Miss Thornton, in the dark of evening. He had parted with Valentine (who had gone in to see his new connections), urging that he had to get to the offices, but he still lingered for a moment and stared gloomily up at the lighted windows of that high and quiet house.

"I ought to be off," he thought. "The time has come now if ever it could, to take my eternal nose out of these people's concerns. Valentine is married, and we all know what that means. A friend (for I really believe there were times when Valentine hoped for my salvation), a friend gone what would be technically termed pop. I have no right to be always dancing in their way: that my soul knoweth right well. I must be gone: I should be gone, but that a snivelling imp of a sentiment had got into me: something I'm ashamed to name. Well, there can't be any harm in staring up at the window, though the sagacity of it might be questioned. After that I will take up my bed and walk ... and, Oh Lord, what a walk up hill it will be." He drew himself up, utterly depressed, and seemed resolute to turn his back on the house.

"Basil! Hulloo!" called out a maddeningly cheery voice, and Howe, turning beheld Lucien advancing, his gleaming teeth grinning from under his hat; and his silver-headed cane swinging loosely in his hand. "Oh, I say, old fellow," he went on, laughing apologetically,

"I am so glad to have you here to enliven me. I was feeling deuced low and wretched." Here he took Howe's arm, a gesture particularly repugnant to that gentleman, who always had an odd respect for the person of his companion, down to the smallest child, but to which motion he made no resistance. "I say, you're jolly always: do you ever have the blue devils? I've got them now."

"Well," said Howe, with effort, followed by a clear and even sympathetic tone, "will you tell me why his Satanic Majesty has sent his cerulean legionaries to you just now. What is the matter, Lucien?"

"Oh, I don't know whether you'd understand," began Lucien with the same nervous laugh. "The fact is ... that is, would you laugh at me very much if I said I was in love?"

"Why should I?" said Howe, mildly. "I should have to be engaged in laughing at a very large proportion of the human race, if that were the case. I should like to ask you, Lucien," he said, lowering his voice, for the first time in Lucien's experience, with something like earnestness, "whether you see any reason in it, for me to hurt your feelings."

"Oh no," said Lucien, readily, "only I thought perhaps you –. But the fact is, it's like this. You know Miss Gertrude Grey –"

For the first time, I think, in his life, a black surge of ambition rose high in Basil's heart, and seemed madly to bid him clutch ere it was too late. The next moment he despised himself for his weakness, pulled himself together and said bravely, "I know Miss Grey a little: but you know her best."

"I wish I knew what she thought of me," said Lucien, almost hysterically. "The fact is I'm quite off my head about it ..."

"Well, it's better than being on your head," said Howe, comfortingly, for he felt quite compassionate despite his own depression. "I've known times when it's just as well to be a little mad. Have you said anything to Miss Grey?"

"I haven't dared yet," said Lucien, tremulously. "I'm afraid she despises me: and that makes me horribly wretched."

"Oh, I don't think so," said Howe, in a deep reassuring voice. "She has no right to despise you, and from what I have seen of her I shouldn't think she did. Are you really quite serious, Lucien? I mean ... is it a matter of your happiness?"

"Utterly," said Lucien, warmly. "I couldn't live without her. All the good that is in me can only come out with her."

Howe buttoned up his frock coat, as if over the sudden and cruel coldness at his own heart. He remembered his wager with Valentine about the conversion of Lucien and spoke firmly: "My dear fellow, if you want my advice, I don't suppose you do, but here it is. Think honestly and finally about those last words you said. If they are true: then who am I (I really don't quite know who I am, to tell the truth), who am I, who is anyone to deny you a right to feel it and say it. There is no reason, believe me, why you should be in the blues. Your wish is perfectly honest and is often, generally, the best thing in the world that can happen to a person."

"Then," said Lucien, smiling feebly at the darkness, "you advise me to tell her."

"Rather than fret," replied Howe, lit a cigar and put it between his lips, which were quite white.

"You've always been a good cousin to me, Basil," said Lucien, genuinely touched, for Howe's grave manner was very gentle, "and it's very nice to have a cheerful person like you, when one has real sorrows. I'll screw up my courage, to flatter you. I'll tell her now. Good night." He capered off into the growing darkness and the next moment Howe heard a bell ring in the porch.

Just at the same moment something wet fell on Howe's nose.

"Rain," he said. "I wish it would soak me into a pulp like an old hat."

The rain fell faster, but he still paced the wet streets with a new and blank sense of having nowhere to go to. For two hours he drifted through the hissing and gurgling darkness of the high-mansioned neighbourhood and at the end of that time found himself at the same place again. The rain went on falling, cold, ceaseless, blinding as on that day, nearly six years ago when under the twinkling sea-side woods, he had been first dragged into this burning heart tangle to which he was now trying to say a heavy farewell. The life before him was as black as the night, as chill as the rain: he tried to think of a light in it, and could not. He had made his cold bed years before: he must go back to it now. But all this aching press of thoughts only broke through the composed, Red Indian countenance in one sentence:

"I wish rain were drier."

A young man with the least claim to wayward passions and things of that sort would have cursed God and society, but poor Basil Howe only cursed himself, and wondered vaguely whether in some future existence he might be made worthy to catch a glimpse of these lofty natures: Valentine and Catherine and Gertrude. If he had had the consciousness of virtue, he might have been happier, but he never had anything but the consciousness of lunacy. Then he made a sharp effort to face the image of Gertrude finding peace with her old admirer, Lucien, and to be glad of her happiness. He fell back from the effort with a doubt as to its success: in this, in everything he had before him he felt like a man toiling through loose sand.

He puffed stubbornly at his cigar and still the rain fell. It was only the emptiness and darkness around him that gave him leisure to stare at the darkness and emptiness within: occurrences always found him alert. He turned his head at the creak of a gate and braced his weariness to interview another stranger.

"Mr. Howe," said a friendly voice, as an eager face with shadowy red hair was bent out into the dripping darkness. "It is surely not you, out in the rain."

For a second Howe's heart glowed alone in the darkness like the end of his cigar. The next moment it was dull again and his voice came cheerfully through the descending torrents.

"Well, that depends on your definition of rain, Miss Grey. Suppose that I admit that it is, in a certain sense of the word, I: what then?"

"Oh for goodness sake, come in," cried Gertrude in almost angry sympathy. "You must be wet through."

"The comparative want of aridity in my garments," replied he, wringing an end of his soaking mantle, "would seem to fit me more for the outside of a house than the inside."

"Come in, I tell you," said Gertrude imperatively with all the practical wilfulness of a woman, and before Howe fully knew where he was, she had him in the hall and was shutting and bolting the front door.

"Mr. Howe has come in out of the rain," she called out to Margaret, who sauntered out of the library at this point: and taking up the lamp on the hall table, Gertrude marshalled the astonished Howe down the passages into a small dark room at the back of the house, lit only by a dull glowing fire. Into the red twilight of this parlour Gertrude ushered him, set the lamp on the table, stirred the fire to a glare and offered him a seat. He obeyed her in a trance of dizzy, perilous happiness: put out his cigar, hung up the black, high, polished hat: symbol of the dark weight of formalism he had borne so patiently through life, sat down and looked at her. She was moving about the room, humming, the red and tawny lights of the lamp and fire playing about the red and tawny tints of her face and hair: and in her eyes, now at their softest blue, there was a dreamy pleasure as she moved. So far she had simply knocked the senses out of him with the contrast between the darkness, wet and hopelessness, and this glowing room and intoxicating presence. Now he recovered his wits and will and rose.

"Miss Grey," he began.

"You sit down," she observed promptly. "You can't go till the rain has stopped."

"Miss Grey," said Howe, in a stumbling voice, "I ought not to be here.... Lucien ..."

Gertrude paused in adjusting the lamp with a laugh on her lips: "Lucien: did you know he had been here?"

"I heard something of it," said Howe with dry, white lips.

"Poor old Lucien," said Gertrude, with a sort of affection in her tone, "I have just been refusing to marry him.... What is the matter Mr. Howe?"

"Nothing, thank you," said Howe, and rose again, his heart beating in his throat. "Did you say you had refused him.... What was it...?"

"Yes," she replied laughing, "but it wasn't the first time. I believe it was the third time of asking: with intervals of other fair ladies between."

Basil Howe stood opposite to her, and his eyes burnt blue out of his pale face.

"Miss Grey," he said, "do you feel equal to two questions of that kind in one evening?"

Gertrude let the book in her hand slip to the floor and stood, red to the roots of her hair.

Nothing but the sudden and staggering removal of the moral weight of the thought that she belonged to Lucien could have made Basil say this with the terrible calmness that he did. When he realised that he had said it, his conduct was curious. He turned round, took down his hat, threw his cloak over his arm, and said with a tone of utter abasement: "Give me the answer, Miss Grey, and walk me out. I am a fool and I have brought our long experiment to a close." And he stepped towards the door slowly.

"Mr. Howe," said Gertrude, "you may hang up your hat again." Then in a thoughtful voice to herself, "It is true what he says.... It is something very like it ... friendship, love, what shall we call it... it bears that name better."

Howe, with the huge calm of his most entire triumphs of self-decision, passed on towards the door and put his hand on the handle. Gertrude seemed to realise that he was going with a sudden horror, like one starting from a dream.

"Basil!" she cried, loud and sudden, and that word only of all words made him turn his head. For he knew that old friends as they were, she had never called him so before. Something in her face, almost hectic in its sudden excitement, made him slowly retrace his steps, and the two stood face to face.

"Wait a moment, Basil," she said softly. "I have something to tell you: a long story told shortly."

He went up to the fireplace and leant his arm and head against it: as Gertrude spoke slowly.

"Love is a funny thing, and all the poets write about it and say it's nice."

Even in this strange crisis, her brooding companion could not repress a half-laugh at this singularly abstract beginning.

"Love as most people understand it," went on Gertrude thoughtfully, "is a very beautiful and necessary sort of thing, but it is the wildest toss-up that the genius of man ever devised. People who meet and fall in love, as dear Catherine did with Valentine: people who love at first sight, and they are an immense majority, see each other, I will not say falsely, but poetically and vaguely: they are each a sort of beatific vision to the other. I suppose it is a good thing that God should have instituted this healthy delusion to give young people a start in their interest in humanity, should tie this delightful bandage over eyes that might grow too inquisitive and cynical: but it is the merest cant in the world to pretend that it is not so: or that lovers do know each other in any practical sense of the word. They do not: they see 'a visible god': and there is an end of it."

Gertrude bit her mittens a minute before she proceeded with her strange lecture. She knew well that Howe was listening, though she did not look at him. Then she went on in a lower voice. "But there is a kind of love: a love that comes to two now and then:

that is different: the love that is knowledge. The love that in some time, most likely the dark unconscious hours of childhood, springs up in a companionship, in a constant interchange of feelings, a constant mutual influence. Years may pass, separations for nearly a decade may come between, quarrels even and jealousies, but those two will know each other till the crack of doom: they will only have to look across at each other, and they will see all secrets in each other's eyes, as plainly as if in words: the bond between them will not, cannot be untied by either. A meaning they will always have to each other, a power over each other, because they have, at some period, looked literally into each other's hearts, in some great hour of confession. That is love indeed: but it comes only to a few ... to a few."

Howe lifted his face, and it was awful, as of a man that had been held dumb before the face of God.

"You and I," he said, with low accents of a sudden and vivid enlightenment. "You and I: on the stone pier by the sea, you and I; in the old woods and along the old sea-cliff, you and I. In the ballroom and the conservatory, at the tea-table with dozens of others – you and I. Across the void of blankness of six years, and in the bewildering quadrille, you and I. In the paradise of Valentine's love, and in the church of God where he was married, you and I. There was never anything else in life – but you and I."

Then there was a long, dark silence, and the fire spluttered in the grate. Then at last Howe spoke again, and his unwonted tragedy of note had vanished, and he said, abruptly:

"Miss Grey ... I never was different ... Could you put up with me, do you think? Oh, I wish I were more worth your while." And his head bowed a little, as he took both her hands.

Gertrude came nearer as his head sank lower and lower, and kissed him on the forehead barred and troubled with long restlessness, ingenuity, loneliness; which that one kiss, pure and brave as her own heart, put to rest at last. And the kiss also was Gertrude's last confession.

"Dear me," said Miss Thornton, with undulation, "Gertrude going to marry Mr. Howe ... well ... well, he'll keep her amused at any rate."

This seemed to be the view of the match taken by the world in general, with which both parties are popular. It may be noticed, however, that whenever anyone (Mr. Lucien Fleury, for instance, who married and lived happily with Miss Marjory Amiens): that when anyone gave expression to this light and jocular view of their relationship and its merits, the eyes of the two would meet, and they would offer something or do each other some small kindness, as if they were alone together. The world, which they are far from despising, does not make any deductions from this. They think it is part of the humour.

The End

The Chesterton Society

If you wish to join the Chesterton Society and receive *The Chesterton Quarterly*, please send your full name and address plus your subscription to:

The Treasurer,
The Chesterton Society,
107 Hartington Road,
Brighton BN2 3PA.

Current annual subscription rates are: UK £12.50; student concessionary rate £5.00; overseas US $30 (or the equivalent in sterling). Standing orders can be made to The Chesterton Society, Account No 30-18-16, 07069066, Lloyds TSB Bank, Brighton, England. Any change in subscription will be subject to debate at the Annual General Meeting and will be notified through the columns of *The Chesterton Quarterly*.